Hunky Nerd 1 & 2

Hunky Nerd Series, Volume 2

Jordan Rivers

Published by A. I. Rivers, 2024.

HUNKY NERD 1 & 2

First edition. April 19, 2024.

Copyright © 2024 Jordan Rivers.

ISBN: 979-8224395170

Written by Jordan Rivers.

Table of Contents

CHAPTER 1: HIS STORY...1

Chapter 2...7

Chapter 3...13

Chapter 4...20

CHAPTER 5: HER STORY..21

Chapter 6...26

Chapter 7...33

Chapter 8...36

Chapter 9...43

BONUS | HUNKY NERD 2: CHLOE & DAEVON 47

CHAPTER TWO: CHLOE & DAEVON 55

CHAPTER THREE: CHLOE & DAEVON 62

CHAPTER FOUR: CHLOE & DAEVON..............................70

CHAPTER FIVE: CHLOE & DAEVON.................................78

To all the ladies out there who are fulfilling their dreams and setting their own course.

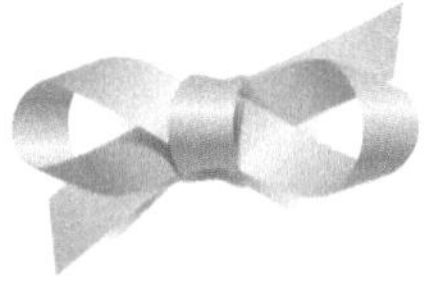

CHAPTER 1: HIS STORY

I headed my Harley onto Mulholland Drive among the Hollywood hills as I traveled on my way to my next client. My helmet and leathers – all black – baked in the California sun, but that was a lot better than taking the chance of flying off the bike and choosing road rash in place of your skin. And while I know I'm a nice-looking guy, not even a hobbit would choose road rash over natural skin.

Leaning my Harley Springer into the curves of Mulholland, I was happy that my rich client was up here because you haven't lived until you've ridden a Harley up here with all the twists and turns of the road. Of course, I would have preferred going faster, but what are you gonna do? There's always some slow poke just around the next curve, and I don't fancy slamming into the back of a Mercedes and flying overhead until I crash-landed or something tall stopped me suddenly.

I'm a tech guy. I've built my own business from the ground up since I was sixteen. Now, ten years later, I work when I want, where I want and who I want to work with. I did the travel thing, going around the world to exotic places and working in other countries, but I always came back to California and the good old U-S- of -A. Since I can afford to live here, Cali offers me everything I need, with great weather most of the time. And the traffic doesn't bother me. I just weave my bike in and out of it and get to where I'm going long before anybody else. But I have to keep my eyes open for rich assholes who are suffering from road rage from sitting in total gridlock for hours. They watch you coming up in between the traffic – which is legal in So Cal – and throw open their car door so you slam into it and go splat! They can afford the insurance hit and just claim they were opening their door to get out to see what was holding everything up traffic-wise. Trust me, I'm prepared to tuck and roll at any moment.

I pull up to the tall gates at my client's address. The house is set so far back off the road that you can't see it due to the curve in the road. I flip up my helmet's visor and hit the call button mounted on the metal pole next to the driveway. There's a camera staring at me from about the call button, and I scan the area while I wait for my client, R Walker, to answer. There are two more cameras mounted high on either side of the gate walls. The service that screens my calls and sets up my appointments using a pre-requisite that I have established lets me know only that R Walker has a technology home that runs everything. Opening and closing things. Turning lights off and on. Adjusting temperature and humidity. Watering the garden, cleaning the pool, and probably even wiping their ass. But who am I to make fun? This is my business, fixing all the computer shit that goes bad. I should be grateful - and I am. It's just that, lately, I've grown restless. I can't put my finger on what it is. I know what's going on in other places, on other shores. It's not like I can't hop on a plane and go anywhere at a moment's notice. I dunno. I just want – something.

"Hello, may I help you?"

My head snaps back to the speaker on the pole. The voice that came out of that box was like sexy smoke rising and slowly curling upwards. And that's saying something coming out of that kind of speaker. For the first time in a long time my cock sat up and took notice. I usually get a good buzz from the vibration between my legs that my Harley gives me, but this was something else.

"Yeah, Alex McCall, the tech you called to fix your computer modules."

As if in answer, the gates began to slowly swing open. I slap the visor back down onto my helmet, put my Harley into gear, and speed up the drive. I had to get a look at the maid or assistant or whomever it was that belonged to that incredible, erection-producing voice. I was just hoping it wasn't old man R Walker's trophy wife. No touchy the client's wife – or any man's wife for that matter. They may be beautiful, but in this town, that will get you killed. Or at least your business ruined.

If you want to be around beautiful women – move to California. Southern California specifically. Los Angeles/Beverly Hills/ Hollywood/Santa Monica/Newport Beach – you get the idea. No matter how beautiful a woman looks in another state, there are one hundred more just like her here. If you've won a beauty contest and people tell you to go to So Cal and be a model or an actress, prepare yourself. There are hundreds of contest-winning beautiful women out here. Same with the men. Tons of GQ guys everywhere. All vying for the same few modeling and acting roles that are here. That's why they are all – men and women – working other jobs to support themselves while they are waiting for that Big Break. It's a standing joke out here that all waiters and waitresses are really actors. But waiting tables is the only job that you can work around while you hit all the auditions. And, of course, if you land something, you can walk away from waiting tables because once your gig is finished, there's always another waiter or waitress job out there.

Next up is the Trophy Wife. If you can't make it as an actress or a model, you marry for money. It beats going back home as a failure. To make it here, you need to be young, beautiful, and pretty much have big tits. All that acting, modeling and trophy wife stuff keeps all the plastic surgeons busy in this town. Striving for perfection, whether it's for the screen or the social scene, is one of the number one pastimes in So Cal.

Pulling up to the cathedral-like front doors, I turn off my bike, put down the kickstand, and remove my helmet. I swing my leg off the bike and plant my helmet between the handlebars. I pull down the zipper on my leather jacket to allow some cooler air in because I'm already hot and bothered. I wouldn't want to jump the maid, secretary, assistant, or – for god's sake – the butler when they answer the door. Taking off my jacket and laying across my bike, I pull my work satchel out of one of my saddlebags and put the strap over my head and across my chest to hang it at my side.

I ring the front doorbell.

I'm glad I'm wearing my muscle shirt, not just because it keeps me cooler under my leathers, but I also work out religiously like so many others in L.A. that I know I'm sporting two good-sized guns - my arms, in case you do not know the vernacular. I've got that perfect So Cal body with the big chest, large guns, washboard abs, small hips, and tight buns. Not that I'm bragging or anything. I just know that I'm something women like because they usually come on to me. I've never really had to work for it.

The door finally swings open, and the most incredible-looking raven-haired beauty has answered it. Dressed in a black cashmere sweater tucked into grey slacks, she has a slamming body. Nice, high breasts whose décolletage peaks out of the V-neck of her sweater. She has a small waist and a flat stomach, as if she's never had kids. But – hey – this is Hollywood; they have surgeries for that. She's older than me. I can tell by the wisdom in her eyes and the way she holds herself. Her face isn't lined heavily, and there are not a lot of laugh lines around her lips or eyes. Her skin is beautiful. Her hair is long and shiny. But she's also not one of those Hollywood socialites. She may take very good care of herself, but instinct tells me that she's the one in power here. She not wielding her "old man's power, pretending it's hers. There's no "Do you know who my husband is?" going on here.

"You're a young one, but you come highly recommended. C'mon in," she says, and trust me, that voice makes me want to follow her anywhere. But I put a tight restraint on the man-whore in me and put on my professional armor. Something tells me that she's used to getting hit on all the time, too, and this was not the time.

"Alex," I offer as I stick out my hand.

"Rachel. Rachel Walker," she smiles politely, and she grasps my hand. Her hand is smaller than mine, but she has a good, solid handshake. I notice that she doesn't have long fake fingernails that seem to be all the rage nowadays. They're clean and clipped straight across as if she does get them manicured regularly. The instant our skin touches, there's a spark. She notices it as well but quickly recovers, letting go of my hand. "I'll show you where the electronics room is," she begins as she turns away from me and starts down a long hallway to the left. The house is amazing. The best money can buy with a nice-sized foyer that leads into a Great Room with a floor-to-ceiling fireplace. I love the stonework around the hearth and up the wall. And the wall on the other side of the room from the fireplace is a floor to ceiling fish tank.

I turn my head to watch where I'm going, only to have my eyes locked on her ass. She has a practiced walk that is meant to gather all male eyes to her, but she doesn't overwork it. She not trying, but my eyes stay on her.

"I understand that a few of your modules are out. Can you describe what's been happening?" I ask, trying to get my head into the game.

"I noticed that I had trouble opening some of the doors." She looked over her shoulder and seemed to appreciate that I was not - at that moment -looking at her ass. I had glanced up at her back to concentrate on what she was saying. She stopped and waited for me to come up beside her, and we continued our walk together. "They're set up pretty much to open on their own when I approach – the doors, I mean - but lately, it's been spotty at best. I took the front door offline so I could get in and out because one day, I got locked inside."

Too soon, we arrived at a door, which Rachel opened with a key, and I followed her inside. There is no signage on the door so as not to make it easy for someone to find her electronics room if they were not familiar with the house. Now, all business, I scan the room and get hard again. This was as good as any system I had ever seen or set up myself. It was like the deck of the Enterprise with various panels for different systems throughout the house. Rachel Walker was rich. Or her husband was. And since most women I had run across didn't get into this type of thing, it was a sure bet that this gorgeous woman belonged to someone who had a hard-on for electronic toys. I thought I knew everyone in the business, but I couldn't think of anyone with a major company that lived at this address.

"I had Eric Mathison install most of this. And a Jimmy Levi did the rest," she intoned as she watched my face take in all the various panels.

"They are both great," I replied as I set down my satchel and sat down at the first panel. I was in search and rescue mode as my fingers began flying across the keyboard.

"Some of the cameras and monitors are out as well," she offered.

"I'll get to those too. Don't worry; I'll have you up and running in no time. Eric and Jimmy are great, but I could teach them a thing or two, even though I'm younger than they are."

"No brag, just fact?" she said as she quirked a half smile.

"Something like that," I looked at her and grinned. She seemed to search my eyes with her own and then turned away.

"Well, I'll leave you to it. I'm sure you can find the intercom if you need anything." She paused in the open doorway. "If you get hungry, help yourself to whatever's in the kitchen. There are cold drinks, but you'll find that they are horribly good for you and not anything sugary. There's an ice drawer in the kitchen island and you can drink water out of the tap because I've got a huge filtration system for the house."

"Sounds good," I replied as I kept my eyes on what I was doing. "Thanks. I'm sure I'll be all right." When I didn't hear another word or sound, I turned and looked. But she was gone.

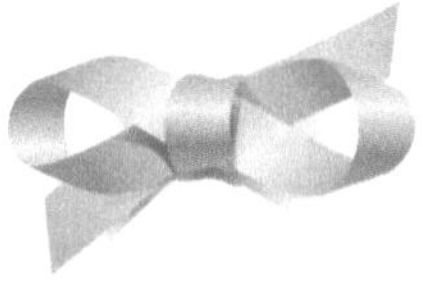

Chapter 2

I was fixing the cameras before too long. I use them to look around the house to make sure everything is in order and working. Rachel has an indoor Olympic-sized pool, a killer weight/exercise room, steam room and sauna, two small hot and cold pools, the kitchen is fit for a chef, there's a formal dining room, lots of empty bedrooms with bathrooms that have deep tubs and separate showers, a two-story library loaded with books and a massive carved wooden desk that sports a large Apple computer and various yellow legal pads with writing, cups of pens and various awards on the dark wood walls.

The next camera image stops me in my tracks. Rachel's bedroom. It is a huge master that seems bigger than the house I grew up in. A vintage Laura Ashley Palas bed with a crown of draperies clothing the four-poster bed is in the center. The bed isn't even hugging a wall. And why do I know who Laura Ashley was? My mother wanted that bed forever and it was the first thing I had gotten her when I started my own business. But it was impossible to find that crown that hung from the gathered four posters because they had stopped making it. But here was a bed that had it.

In the center of the bed, on top of the covers, is Rachel. Her eyes are closed, and she is slowly running her hands all over her body. Without even thinking about it, my hand goes down to my crotch, and I start rubbing myself through my Levi's. Soon, Rachel begins pulling the cashmere free from her slacks, and she unbuttons it without opening her eyes. I zoom the camera in tighter, but not so tight that I can't see most of her form. She has on a black lace bra that shows most of her cleavage, and she starts running her hands all over her breasts.

D-A-M-N! I thought to myself as I rubbed myself through my jeans harder. Soon, Rachel was unclipping the bra at the front closure and spreading it wide.

I nearly swallow my teeth.

Her breasts are perfect. Large but not huge. Natural-looking, not the result of implants. And if they aren't real, her surgeon deserves a fucking award. The nipples have large, dark areolas, high and erect with excitement. Just like my cock is. And when she strokes her breasts, her mouth falls open with pleasure.

I grab the top of my button-fly Levi's and rip them open with one pull. My cock springs out through the slit in my boxers and is already crying for release, a clear purl of liquid resting at the tip.

Rachel begins gently rolling her nipples between her fingers, back and forth, and she really likes it. Her hips start to grind gently, and she is worrying her bottom lip with her teeth. Finally, she sits up and pulls off her sweater and bra and tosses them to the floor. She shimmies out of her slacks and lets them join her other clothes. Leaving her black lace panties on, she lays back down and goes back to cuddling and kneading her breasts. As I take hold of my cock – "Fuck!" I bark out. I am so ready to explode, and she is just at her breasts. I pray she continues to explore everything that God has given her.

As if reading my mind, she slides one hand down her smooth flat belly until it gropes her sex through her panties. She tosses her head back deeper into her pillow and the hand that is kneading her breast starts twisting the nipple again. This causes her long legs to rub together. I don't know how she is still holding on since I'm about to blow the top of my cock off. I frantically search around for a container. I don't want to juice all over the control panels and possibly short them out. Of course, if that meant I could stay here longer – shit – and just how would I explain that? I remember my stainless-steel mug in my satchel and dig for it while watching everything Rachel is doing on the monitor.

Finally, unable to stand it another moment, Rachel whisks off her panties and sends them flying. She spreads her legs wide, bringing her knees up and out. She then opens the lips by spreading two fingers from one hand like an upside-down peace sign before dipping the middle finger of the other hand into her juicy folds and pulling all that gleaming wetness up to her little bead at the top of her mound. She rubs faster and faster. I have the empty – thankfully clean – mug in one hand while I am fisting my cock with the other. As I explode hard at the exact same moment as Rachel does, I place the mug over the top of my cock to catch the hot jets that pour out of me like I have never climaxed before. Both Rachel and I are moaning and gasping loudly. She finally collapses and lay there spread out like a feast still to be enjoyed. My cock is still pumping like it has reserves of glossy fluid. I have already stopped stroking it, hoping to get it to stop.

Finally, I reach down and give my balls a gentle squeeze and see stars. I am now collapsed. It is everything I could do to put the mug on the side shelf of the panel, so I won't dump it onto the floor. I close my eyes and just listen to my breathing finally returning to normal along with the rhythm of my heart which had seemed to want to burst out of my chest when I came. I thought back over the course of my life since I had lost my virginity, trying to remember a time I had ever volcano-ed that hard, but couldn't. Opening my eyes, I look at the monitor. Rachel is gone. Her clothes are missing too. I quickly stuff myself back into my boxers and button up the front of my pants. I don't want her to walk in here and find me like this, especially with the monitor fixed on her bed.

Shutting off all the cameras as though they had not been fixed yet, I turn to other matters that need attention. I don't know how long I worked, but I was suddenly hungry. I rise from the chair and stretch. Rachel had mentioned that I could raid the fridge. I then catch sight of that mug and remember it has a lot of milky juice in it. I'd better find a sink and rinse it out before she asks about it. Having already explored the house through the monitors, I have a pretty good idea where the kitchen is, so I grab up my satchel and the mug and stride off. Along the way, I admire the house, the furnishings, and the open feeling that a house this size is able to offer.

As I enter the kitchen, I freeze. Rachel is cooking. She has all kinds of ingredients on a massive center island with a wooden cutting board as its surface. In the very middle is an eight-burner stove, and the far end has a small sink. It smells like red meat and chicken are cooking.

"Hi," Rachel greeted me with a beautiful smile on her face. "Hungry?"

Oh, yeah, I am hungry, all right. I'm just not sure if food will be able to satisfy me after seeing her climax so hard. She is wearing a loose-fitting dress that falls to her feet – which are bare. I think I had heard of those dresses referred to as moo-moos. On her, the tropical print encouraged all kinds of jungle images of me playing Tarzan to her Jane. As soon as I allowed myself to wonder if she was totally naked under that shift, my cock was back on the "Hi, how are you?" train.

"I could eat, yeah," I smile back as I set my satchel down. Going to the farmer's kitchen sink behind her, I turn on the water and begin washing out my mug.

"Are you all finished?" she inquires with a sudden expression of worry as she turns to look at me.

I don't want her to think that I have finished everything and may have caught her little exercise session. "No. I still have the cameras to do, and then I'll be out of your hair in no time." I leave the clean mug upside-down in her sink.

"No hurries. You've been working for quite a while. Relax. Want a beer?"

"Yeah, a beer sounds great. But I thought you didn't have anything unhealthy in here?"

Rachel brings back two cold bottles and hands one to me. "I only buy organic beer. Hope that's okay," she smiles as she twists off her cap.

"Fine by me," I grin as I twist off my cap and scan the label. It tastes so cold and delicious going down. I set my bottle on the kitchen island and sat on one of the stools in front of it.

"Fajitas, okay?" she asks as she continues with her cooking.

"Love 'em. Mexican food and beer. You trying to wrangle a cheaper bill out of me?"

Rachel laughs as I had intended. Her laughter is like music to my ears, and I find myself wanting to hear it more often. She is softer and more relaxed now. I don't know if it is due to her little sex play or that I was righting everything in her electronic world, or if she is just getting used to me. I am hoping it is just me, but hey, I'm a realist.

It isn't long before we are both perched on the stools enjoying our homemade fajitas, guacamole, and salsa. The sour cream seems to be the only thing that came out of a container, as Rachel apprises me that she had made the tortillas herself. She goes on to tell me that she had taken a cooking class a few years back when she was going through a bored streak, and that had helped spice things up considerably, both literally and figuratively.

"So, what do you do for a living? If you don't mind me asking?" I ask as I make my third helping of fajitas, combining the steak and chicken.

"I'm a novelist."

"And a very good one by the looks of this place," I intone.

"I got lucky. I do a series about female vampires, and it's really big with the women."

"What? No male vamps?" I tease before taking another mammoth bite of my almost-gone fajitas and contemplating my fourth.

"They think they're all gone. So, they must get with human men."

"And do they mind 'getting' with human men?"

"They make do."

"Ouch!" I fake an arrow taking out my heart which causes Rachel to laugh again. "I feel as if I should defend my sex somehow."

"Help me clean up the kitchen, and we'll call it even."

"You're on!" I laugh, and we both keep eating.

Chapter 3

We are done cleaning up the kitchen, one of the two dishwashers is running, Rachel is drying her hands, and I am beginning to think I'd better get back to my work because it is getting late. Or pretend to get back to work since I am already finished.

"So," Rachel begins as she hangs up the colorful kitchen towel on a rack at the side of the kitchen island. "You have a toolbelt in that satchel?"

"Yeah, I use one sometimes when I have to climb poles or need more than one tool and there's not always a table or a platform to lay my tools on."

"Can I see it?"

Shrugging, I lean down and bring my satchel onto the kitchen island. I flip the flap over and unzip it. It's the work of a moment to pull it out and hold it up for her.

"No, I mean, can I see you with it on?" She is holding her bottom lip with her teeth. My cock remembers the last time that she did that. What she was physically doing when her teeth were doing that. I put the belt on and held my hands up to show her. "Well, don't you have to have tools in it for it to be a toolbelt?" She crossed her arms in front of her chest as she gave me a look that said, "Duh." This is getting weird, but of course, Rachel can ask me to do just about anything and I will. I fill the belt with the tools and move out from the island so I am facing her. We are both standing between the island and the sink.

"Take off your shirt."

Instantly, my body goes nuclear hot. I am already dressed in a muscle shirt and jeans. If she wants my shirt off when she can already see so much of me, this is going in a direction I never want to return from. I whip off my shirt and drop it to the floor and just wait, panting.

"Your boots next."

The boots come off.

Do I have to tell you the rest?"

"Yes," I reply, "I want you to tell me everything you want."

"I want you to make love to me on this kitchen island."

Trust me when I say the only thing that stayed on was the toolbelt. I have her up on that counter and the dress off in a heartbeat. She has on nothing but those black lace panties. My jeans were long gone, and we were kissing in a slow, sensual manner that made my head spin. I make sure to pay loving attention to her lips. Kissing, licking, gently biting, and kissing again. She keeps trying to grab my cock, but I keep redirecting her hands to my shoulders.

When I finally push my tongue inside those gorgeous lips, she is so ready that she starts sucking on my tongue. My hands go through her soft hair and make their way down to her shoulders, where I smooth my hands all over them. I knead them gently, hold her by the neck as I kiss her and French her repeatedly. I kiss her eyelids, her nose, her cheeks and pull her earlobes gently with my teeth. My hands smooth down her spine, and I massage and stroke her back, knowing I am driving her crazy because I'm not touching the usual places that she expects me to rub.

"God damn it! Suck my tits!" she moans as her head lulls back.

"No," I tease as I nibble her throat and collar bones, my big shoulders a barrier to her hands finding my cock. If she did find it, this whole thing would be over, and I am planning on this being the most shattering and memorable sex she has ever had. By now, she is practically lying across the clean cutting board; only my arms along her back keep her up.

Finally, I arch her back up and put her breasts right in my face. They are soft and pliant; I nuzzle them with my face. Her moaning is low and continuous in my ears. I remembered her stretched out on her bed, playing with her breasts, rolling her nipples, her mouth dropping open in pleasure as if someone were sucking on her nipples. I gently take the first one in my lips and tongue the tip. Rachel starts writhing and moaning louder. Teasing them with my teeth drives her even more crazy, and then I suck them.

She. Came. Hard.

I gently lay her on the countertop and move my arms out to the side of her, leaning on them while I watch her experience her pleasure, her hands on my biceps. Her eyes are closed; she is panting and gasping as little shutters go through her body. It is a while before she slowly opens her eyes. They are glassy and not too focused. She gently squeezes both of my biceps at the same time as if in 'thank you'. Her brain comes back online, and she focuses on my face.

"Thank you," she murmurs.

"My pleasure," I whisper with a smile.

"No, I mean, thank you for letting me enjoy it instead of insisting on getting inside me immediately. I've never had a man do that for me before."

"Again, my pleasure," I whisper and gently kiss her lips.

"Now I need you to fuck me hard. Not that I didn't love what you just did, but I don't want you to die from blue balls and I need to feel you inside me."

I throw back my head and laugh and she takes that opportunity to grab my cock. I almost jack-knife back toward the sink. She uses both of her hands on my cock to pull me back to her. Now I am the one panting and moaning. My cock is as hard as steel from waiting so impatiently, but now all bets are off. If I don't get inside her immediately, her hands are going to be full of my hot juice. I push her back down, freed my cock from her grip and spread her long legs wide. I slam into her because I am already starting to shoot. She is more than ready. Her own hot juices make her slick and ready. We both shout out loud at the joining. I can't believe how tight she is. I grab her hips and pull her toward me as I slam into her. She wraps her legs around my ass. Rachel's back is supported by the counter, and I pistoned into her as my hot squirts stream into her over and over again.

She crescendos again, and I can't seem to stop. My head is spinning. I finally have to stop, and I lean in against her and put my arms back on the counter. I am panting like I don't run six miles a day. And that little minx smiles at me like a Cheshire cat.

"Let's do that again," she purrs.

"Your wish, my command."

Throwing her up over my shoulder, I stride off toward what I hope is her bedroom, betting she will correct my course if necessary. Rachel shrieks in surprise and begins giggling.

Giggling.

I love it. She reaches down and swats my ass, and I turn my head and gently bite her ass.

"Left! Left!" she cries as I take a wrong turn, and we are soon in her huge master bedroom. I kick the door shut and toss her onto the bed. As she bounces, she laughs and opens her arms to me. She is so beautiful. I climb onto her bed and into her arms, stroking that soft skin. Trust me when I say the toolbelt is long gone.

"Please tell me – now that some sanity has returned – that there is no husband that's going to be bursting through the bedroom door at any moment," I grin, only half kidding.

"That would be awkward," Rachel laughs as she tosses her raven hair. "But, no, no husband or boyfriend. Not even a frenetic fan stalking me."

"Now, that, I find hard to believe, considering how many crazy people there are out there in the world - especially in L.A." We both laugh and begin kissing again. This time she takes a hold of my cock quickly and rolls me to my back as she looms over me like the wild cat she is. She settles between my legs, stroking my cock and balls. She really examines them as her soft hands explore every inch of me. And trust me, there is a lot to explore. Before I know it, her mouth is on my balls slowly sucking one in and playing with it with her tongue. Then she pops that one out, pulling as she goes, and my eyes roll into the back of my head. She sucks the next one in and does the same thing. My cock is standing up and saluting in the name of God, Country, and Raging Sex.

Then my eyes shoot back forward and down because she is licking the head of my cock. Her tongue swirls around and slides through the crease at the top of my head. She double-hands my shaft and gently begins twisting and stroking, her hands going in opposite directions.

"F-u-c-k!" I breathe, the sensations she is creating in my cock, balls and belly climbing out of control. Mount Vesuvius was a firecracker compared to my cock exploding. And she is right there, her mouth sucking me in and swallowing every drop that explodes out of me. I am laid to waste. My limbs and body are putty as I just lay there, my bones no longer solid. She waits until my eyes look at her again and she licks her Cheshire cat lips. I gather her into my arms, and we hold each other. We're quiet for a long time.

"So, should we call it a night?" she queries as she looks up at me.

"Never!" I whispered vehemently. Rolling on top of her, I begin kissing her again like I had in the kitchen. It doesn't take long for her moans to fill the room and mine join hers because this time I don't keep her away from my cock. Soon I'm kissing my way to her breasts, and I take those nipples between my fingers the way I had seen her do it. I gently roll them back and forth as I lick up her sternum and softly bite those beautiful breasts. Her legs begin sawing and I spend some time kissing her belly button and my hands gently knead her breasts. I know better than to treat her nipples like radio nobs as if I'm using them to try to tune in an F-M station.

I finally lift her legs over my back and settled my face between her thighs, so I am up close and personal with her beautiful, second pair of lips. It is perfect like a peach. Completely free of any hair so I knew I wouldn't be picking any out of teeth later. Her slit glistens with her excitement and, her moans reveal that I am driving her crazy, I take one long lick of her clit from bottom to top.

"Oh, God!" she gasps loudly. So, I do it again. And again. And soon I'm eating that incredible peach, it juices covering my mouth, chin, and nose. Reaching up with my left hand, I encircled her leg and came down from the top of her sex and used two fingers to spread those lips wide. And while I continued to tongue her, my right hand came up from under her and I slid two fingers into that hot wet slit and finger-fuck her. She is screaming my name repeatedly, but I can tell she just can't get over that last hump to bring her to climax, so I use the thumb on the hand that is finger fucking her and slide it into her ass. The guttural scream she gasps out tells me that, not only did she climax hard, but it was probably the hardest explosion of her life. I don't move. Nor did I remove any of my fingers. She shutters and twitches as she comes back down from those enthralling heights of pleasure she had been catapulted into. Suddenly, she begins to cry. That nasty, ugly, cry that women hate men to see, and men hate to see because they don't know what to do. Usually, it sends most men scurrying for the hills. I remove my fingers and take her in my arms, pull the comforter from the bottom quarter of the bed and put it over both of us. I don't say anything. Knew I didn't have to speak a word. She was at her most vulnerable now.

I thought about the first time I'd had sex. I was sixteen and initiated by a friend of my mother's. No, my mom never found out. I always felt like I had been lucky. Instead of trying to lose my cherry by popping some high school girl's cherry, I was brought into 'manhood' by an experienced woman. No birth control issues. A woman that made sure that I understood what was going through women's heads during various sex acts and their expectations. That's probably why I preferred older women. The younger ones don't know what they want. They play games. They're all about the 'slam-bam-thank-you-ma'am' because most guys don't invest any time in the experience, so they think that's the way they have to be too. And they go down on you like, 'Okay, let's just get this over with.' And they don't know how to make love to a man. Men and women both treat sex like it's a game of numbers. How many can you hook up with? Having sex in bathrooms at night clubs never interested me. Hell, night clubs never interested me. There is so much more to the world.

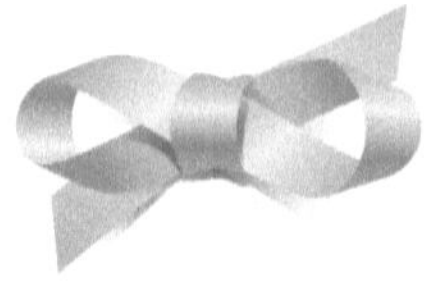

Chapter 4

When I wake the next morning, I'm not sure where I am. This isn't a new experience by any stretch of the imagination. But it has been so long since I was with a woman I am getting used to waking up in my own place. I turn my head and find Rachel grafted to my side, my arm around her warm body. I don't want to move, but I have another appointment that I have to get to, and I don't even know what time it is. I gently remove her from me, and she turns over in her sleep and faces away from me. I make sure she is covered before I leave the room, heading toward the kitchen in search of my clothes.

The automatic everything is working perfectly. The curtains have opened throughout the house. I notice the sprinklers are on outside as I pass a window, and I can smell coffee brewing in the kitchen. I dress and return my tools and my tool belt to my satchel before helping myself to a cup of java which I pour into my stainless-steel mug. And, damn, it was good coffee. So were the memories the mug reminded me of as I linger over the coffee, but I have a schedule to keep. I have six miles to run, a workout to do before a shower, and a change of clothes before hitting my next appointment. I am torn between waking Rachel and letting her sleep. I finally write a note and leave it next to the coffee pot. Grabbing my things, I let myself out the automatic front door – because I now knew the codes – and I went to my bike. It's a good thing I am in So Cal because I had left my leather jacket sitting on my bike all night. I would have been pissed if it had rained. Climbing onto my Harley, I look back at the house one last time before heading toward the front gates.

CHAPTER 5: HER STORY

I'm throwing a pencil straight up into the air, dreaming about the old days when I was in school, and we used to toss a pencil up until it impaled the ceiling. It was stupid, of course, but I was a teenager. We were all teenagers back then. But the really stupid thing is me doing it now. Not only because I'm an adult but also because my ceiling is two floors above my head. I'd probably take out an eye before ever nearing the ceiling target.

But I am bored.

I'm in the middle of my latest vampire book – sixteen in the series – and I just don't want to write. But I can't blow this chicken coup because I am expecting a nerd to show up at the front door. My third nerd in a year. You see, I have a beautiful house that I had designed on paper before turning it over to the pros to have it turned into real architectural plans so it could become a reality. And one thing I really wanted was a house that anticipated my needs by opening doors as I approached, turned on the coffee, sending the robot floor cleaner out to do its job, and opening and closing the curtains with the rise and fall of the sun, handle the temperature and humidity, run all the cameras in every room, nook and cranny watching out for intruders, etc. I grew up watching all the Star Treks, so sue me. The problem is that the first nerd recommended to me to design the system and put everything into motion, couldn't concentrate around me. He'd mumble instead of speaking. He'd drop things and literally freak out. The second nerd leered at me constantly. I understand that their large brain makes them short on social graces, but please! Someone give these kids a mercy fuck so they can handle being around women. Needless to say, I didn't volunteer, and the first two didn't last. I am now on my third nerd. Hey, that rhymes. He comes highly recommended. Someone who can handle being around women employers.

I put the pencil away in my desk drawer. I never write with pencils – I hate to, in fact. I only use pens, several of which are scattered all over my desk, along with all the yellow legal pads that I jot on. Facts, figures, dialogue, and doodles. I'm dressed in what I feel is professional attire, a black cashmere sweater with gray slacks. Hey, don't give me a hard time; my air conditioning is on.

I wander over to the two-story window that makes up one wall of my office. I have two stories of bookshelves that are filled to the brim and a silly corkscrew staircase that leads to the second floor - even though it's considered bad Feng Shui. My awards are all over the walls, along with clusters of pictures here and there of my friends, me getting awards, my special nights, etc. I've lived alone pretty much most of my life and never found it lonely. However, lately, I'm feeling restless and very lonely.

The gate bell goes off.

I stroll over to the monitor and see that whoever it is has arrived on a Harley-Davidson. Not quite geek transportation. It's probably some actor going to what they think is an audition in the Hollywood Hills only to wind up drunk or stoned and used as a sex toy by a bunch of fat-bellied degenerates posing as producers. And maybe they really are producers, but that guy would never get the part after they used him up.

"Hello, may I help you?" I ask. His head whips around and he looks straight into the camera. "Wow," I say out loud even though I am alone. Just the face gazing out of the helmet is handsome as hell. Great jaw. High cheekbones. And those blue eyes...

"Yeah, Alex McCall, the tech you called to fix your computer modules," he answers in a deep voice that was like velvet in my ears. This can't possibly be 'the nerd' I ordered. Feeling stupid for just staring, I slap the button below the monitor that opens the gate. Boy, I must have him check the heater too. Either that or I just got a major hot flash. And suddenly, I notice that I'm feeling wet between my legs. Outside of the shower or bathtub, that hasn't happened lately. Removing my high heels, I run for the front door. Once there, I'm grateful that the door isn't automatically opening because I need to slow down my breathing and put my shoes back on.

The doorbell rings.

I pull myself together and put on my best 'professional' face and open the front door. He's standing there in a muscle shirt with plenty of muscles to show off. He's wearing jeans and boots. He has sandy blond hair down past the nape of his neck, and it's been cut in that 'devil-may-care' manner that usually doesn't work off the movie screen, but he wears it well.

Damn, I think to myself as I resist the urge to give him the twice over. Again. *There ought to be fucking be a law...* I lament to myself. But suddenly I realize that this hunk probably has women lined up the block, already on their backs with their legs spread wide for him. He's got that look about him that says he knows how good he looks, and he probably never has had to chase a female. He probably rides a Harley so he can get away if they pool into the mob. A man could get ravished to death. But, hey, this is Hollywood, I remind myself. He's probably gay.

"You're a young one, but you come highly recommended," I intone soberly, my initial rush of excitement chilled out with the gay conjecture. "C'mon in."

He steps in, and he's at least six-foot-three. With the boots? Six-five. His head quickly swivels around the foyer before coming back to me. He's so gorgeous, I want to cry. *Gay, gay, gay, gay, gay*, I repeat over and over to myself.

"Alex," he rumbles with that deep voice and sticks out his hand.

"Rachel. Rachel Walker," I smile politely as I shake his hand, making it as firm as I can because I can't stand limp handshakes, but also because his hand is so much bigger than mine. It feels a bit rough, too, as if he does spend some time working with his hands that doesn't involve computers.

Electricity. He notices, too, as we pull our hands apart.

"I'll show you where the electronics room is," I say as I turn and walk down the left-hand hallway. *'I have a stud in my house, not a nerd. Of course, he's gay. I could never get that lucky. Hell, if he's straight, he's probably got a disease. You don't just jump into bed with a guy because he's pretty. He's not pretty, he's handsome. Oh, no-you-don't! Tell that little whore who has suddenly awakened from her slumber that he's gay.* A running dialogue has overtaken my brain as I lead the way to the electronics room.

"I understand that a few of your modules are out. Can you describe what's been happening?

Against my will my head pivots around so I can look into those blue eyes and watch those full lips as they form words. He's looking right at me and not my ass. *See, gay, gay, gay, gay, gay, gay,* I think to myself. I stop and wait for him to catch up to me which takes only a moment for those long legs. *I bet they are as muscular as his arms. Gay or not, I can look, can't I?*

"I noticed that I had trouble opening some of the doors. They're set up pretty much to open on their own when I approach – the doors, I mean – but lately it's been spotty at best. I took the front door offline so I could get in and out because one day, I got locked inside."

I take out the key to the electronics room and unlock the door. I walk in and turn around to watch his face as he takes everything in. He is in the zone. It's like football is to regular guys. Short of blowing up the TV, you can't get a guy to notice anything else when a football game is on.

"I had Eric Mathison install most of this. And a Jimmy Levi did the rest," I intone as I watch his face as he looks at all the various panels.

They are both great," Alex replies as he sets down his satchel and sits down at the first panel. His fingers begin flying across the keyboard.

"Some of the cameras and monitors are out as well," I offer.

"I'll get to those too. Don't worry; I'll have you up and running in no time. Eric and Jimmy are great, but I could teach them a thing or two, even though I'm younger than they are."

Thanks for the reminder, I think to myself.

"No brag, just fact?" I ask as a half-smile quirks across my face.

"Something like that," he looks at me and grins with that million-dollar smile.

Gay, I remind myself and then turn away.

"Well, I'll leave you to it. I'm sure you can find the intercom if you need anything." I pause in the open doorway. "If you get hungry, help yourself to whatever's in the kitchen. There are cold drinks, but you'll find that they are horribly good for you and not anything sugary. There's an ice drawer in the kitchen island and you can drink water out of the tap because I've got a huge filtration system for the house."

"Sounds good," he replies as he keeps his eyes on what he's doing. "Thanks. I'm sure I'll be all right."

Chapter 6

"Sylvia? Alex McCall. Spill," I say in my direct fashion over my iPhone.

"Oh, he's delicious, isn't he? Is he working for you? Or are you dating him? You're dating him, aren't you? You spill! I want to know all the gory details! He's such a gorgeous hunk! Muscles for miles! I hear he works out two hours a day in his own gym. He's rich, ya know. Of course - you know! You're dating him!"

"Sylvia, breathe," I say dryly. "I called you for the info, remember?"

"Oh, yes. Okay. He's rich. Invented some kind of software when he was sixteen. Has his own company but likes getting his own hands dirty. Guess he doesn't trust anyone else to do the job. Anyway –

"Is he gay?" I actually hold my breath.

"No," she laughs, "why would I ask if you were dating him if he was gay?"

"Who knows why you say what you say sometimes," I laugh back.

"And guess what?"

"All right, I'll bite. What?" I smiled even though we were talking on our cells and not video.

"He prefers older women. Doesn't like those scrawny thin actresses with the fake basketball-sized tits. And he's picky. He doesn't hit on married women, which absolutely drove Kee-Kee Monihan to distraction when he was working at her house. She literally walked up and sat in his lap bare-assed naked!"

"Oh, my god! What did he do?" I asked, trying to get my jaw to rise to meet the rest of my mouth so I could form the words.

"He stood straight up and dropped her right on her ass!"

"Serves her right," I seethed, not believing that I was feeling jealous. I don't even know the guy. "What happened next?"

"He walked out. Called her old man and told him he wouldn't come back and finish unless Kee-Kee was out of the house! Remember when she went to Bali for two weeks? That's why."

Well, isn't that interesting, I muse? "So, I take it that he doesn't mix business with pleasure."

"Dunno, no one's ever spilled in that regard. But you know most of the women around here are married. Except you. You need a trophy husband because you'll never be a trophy wife."

"I think I'll live," I laugh.

"Nita's son plays racquetball with him. Says he likes strong women who don't play games. I wonder if that includes sexual. Nita's son says Alex traveled the world setting up systems for rich people on their private islands and plantations. Guess the women were all over him. And check this: he doesn't smoke or drink hard liquor, and no one's ever seen him do drugs. Turns down weed hits all the time."

"Mister Perfect, as far as I'm concerned. Are you sure he's not gay?" I ask, noticing that I'm getting more and more hot and bothered.

"So - what - if - he - were?" Sylvia laughs heartily. "As long as he services you the way you want - and you definitely need it done to you - who cares what team he plays for?"

"Goodbye, Sylvia," I return to my dry voice and hang up. I sit there a moment. I know it has been a long time since I have had sex, but I am pretty sure the feeling growing within my body right at this moment is horniness.

I. Am. Horny.

I head for my bedroom. It is probably going to take Alex a while before he gets the cameras working, and I can just switch off the one in my room anyway.

I practically ran into my closed door, forgetting that I had taken it offline when the technology in the house had started acting up. I close the door quietly as if Alex, all the way on the other side of the house in the electronics room, knows what I am up to. I can only shake my head at my silliness. *Why do I feel so guilty? I don't know, just because you're going to be getting off on your toolbelt guy?* I admonish myself.

I go to my closet, which I must open the doors on manually because they are offline. I switch on the lights and start looking for something—I don't know—sexy to put on. I stand there for a few minutes, looking through my wardrobe and the built-in drawers of undies.

What the fuck am I doing?

I am planning on masturbating, not dressing for an actual sexual encounter. I gather up my hair and hold it on top of my head with both hands as I often do when I'm thinking or just plain screw-ball-out-of-my-head-stupid. Marching out of the closet, flipping off the lights, and closing the doors as I go, I get onto the bed and lay on my back. *What now? I feel stupid. Exposed.* But fucking horny is winning out over all of that. So, I close my eyes. Immediately, Alex's muscled, tanned, beautiful form comes into sharp focus. I have always been attracted to a man's guns first. Then his ass. Then the rest of him. And men don't have to be pretty. The fact is, the prettier they are – the less I trust them. Alex IS pretty. But I am just going to put that aside for now.

I begin running my hands up and down my body slowly. I start at the top of my head, travel down my face, spend time on my neck and throat, and cross my arms so I can touch my shoulders and finish going down my arms. Slowly. Very slowly I try to trace out every feeling. Every tingle. Every vibration. Soon enough, I am at my breasts. I pay them a lot of attention. They have always been my Achilles' Heel. I had been so small-breasted when I was a teenager, and the high school boys went saucer-eyed and panting dog over all the girls who had big boobs that it made me feel invisible.

In my early twenties, I was living with a guy who used to tell me that, when it came to breast size, anything over a mouthful was a waste.

And the French supposedly considered that anything that overflowed a champagne glass was in the way. Gratifying notions when you didn't have much. I thought Ryan and I were a good team. We were living together and happy – again, I thought. I had gotten published in my teens and was making a comfy living. Ryan wanted to be an actor, so I supported him while he went to audition after audition. Or so I thought. I followed him one day, hoping that I would be able to watch him audition or at least get a look at his competition. Instead, I watched him walk out of the supposed audition with a big-breasted woman who looked like she could nurse an entire litter of puppies. They went to a sleazy motel down on Sunset and checked in. They were in there for HOURS. He never made love to me that long! What is it about big breasts that make men crazy?

After they left the motel, he took her to Denny's. Guess he had to build his strength back up. I left and went home. I called the landlord and told him Ryan was no longer welcome, called a locksmith to change the locks and threw all his clothes and belongings out on the front lawn. He didn't even bother to knock on the front door and ask for forgiveness. He just called the 'Big Boob' broad, collected his things and left. It was at that point that I decided to buy my own house and never live with or support any man ever again. I've owned several houses since, slowly trading up whenever my writing income rose, always paying cash so I would OWN my home.

About three months after I threw Ryan out, I realized I was missing my periods not because I was upset about what Ryan did but - BECAUSE – of what Ryan and I did. Pregnant and single. It was a good thing my parents were no longer around to find out. They had died in a car accident when I was a teen, and I was granted emancipation due to my writing income. There weren't a lot of relatives to choose from anyway. A social worker checked in on me and reported to the judge who had liberated me until I was eighteen. I guess I was a success story. Now, here I was, pregnant and all by myself. But I knew

I could handle it. And writing from an office in my home would allow to take care of my baby without having to leave and work away from home.

MY BREASTS GOT BIGGER!

The pregnancy fairies brought me these full, swelling, generous C-cup-sized breasts. I couldn't believe it; they actually swayed when I bent down to pick something up. I felt feminine. For the first time in my life, I felt like a girl. And you bet your ass, I played with them. I loved the way they felt. I loved how I looked in my clothes. I - HAD - CLEAVAGE! My nipples and areolas got bigger and darker. I couldn't wait to breastfeed. I bought fancy matching bras and panties to wear on my new body after the baby was born. I was going to dress to the nines, showing off my tits. And I wasn't going to let anyone touch them! I was going to drive all those men crazy with want and desire. A punishment for overlooking me.

And then I lost the baby.

A rupture in my uterus stopped everything cold. I lost the baby and was hospitalized for days due to the massive blood loss. The doctors had explained that, if it were going to happen, it usually happened during labor. Apparently, there was a weak spot in my uterus that couldn't take the weight of the growing baby. It had exploded and expelled the baby into my abdomen. The placenta detached from the uterine wall –

Why? Why am I remembering this? I'm the only person I know who can turn a masturbation session into a trip down nightmare lane. Oh, yeah, the reason my breasts turn me on so much. Years later, I found out that plastic surgeons could transfer fat into your breasts and, better still, within a year, the fat would turn into breast tissue. So instead of having something foreign implanted into your body – like, say, breast implants – you could increase your bust size to a full cup. So - I - did - it. And now, here I am, a very generous C cup, and only me to play with them. But I love them. I love the way they feel when I touch them, the way they move, the way they make me look in my clothes, and, most importantly, the way they make me feel.

I play with my breasts through my sweater until I feel frustrated, so I pull my cashmere sweater out from the slacks and unbutton it without opening my eyes. It is hard enough to keep the mood with my trip down nightmare lane; I don't need to open my eyes and see that I am alone. I get back into the mood.

Soon I unclip my black lace bra's front clasp and reveal my nipples to the air. They tighten and perk up. I knead my breasts the way I wish a man would. When I tweak my nipples, it makes me go wet between my legs. I arch my back as I twist the nipples gently, rolling them back and forth. My mouth opens with a moan, and I start that wave-like pulsing I do with my hips when I want to fuck. It is so good; I began to bite my bottom lip with my teeth. Without opening my eyes, I tear off my cashmere sweater and throw it to the floor. I slide out of my slacks and throw those in the same general direction as the sweater. I'm hot and wet between my legs and my love mound wants airtime. But I know I have to tease it more. Back to my breasts. I want to lick them, to have them licked. I want them to be suckled and gently bitten. I want big, rough hands to massage them so I can feel scratchy, warm fingers and palms enjoying the feel of me as I enjoy the feel of them.

Finally, I slide one hand down my tight belly to my black panties and grip myself through the lacy material. *Fuck!* I say to myself, and I throw my head back deeper into the pillow. *Where's a cock when you need one? Uh, excuse me, right down the hallway on the other side of the house,* my libido informs me. I continue kneading my breast and rolling the nipples, which causes me to rub my legs together, and I massage my mound harder.

Whisking off my panties, I throw my legs up and open wide. I spread my engorged lips apart with my fingers and plunge my middle finger into my hot juice and bring it up to the top of my cleft. My little nub is throbbing hard. As soon as the wet, hot touch of my finger registers, I start to get off, but I rub it anyway. Faster. Faster. I climax so hard it almost hurts. And I am imagining Alex watching me. Him stroking his own cock, getting turned on just watching me. I imagined his cock is huge. Its head is purple with blood, and he rubs his hand up and down like a piston. I imagine him blowing the top off his cock like a gigantic volcano, spewing white lava everywhere – especially on me. His hot jets hit me, my folds, stroking more and more as he travels up my stomach covering me with his hot, sticky cream until he is milking himself all over my breasts. Ah, Heaven.

The. Best. Fuck. Of. My. Life.

When I finally come down to earth, I pull my legs together like a lady and slip off the side of the bed closest to my clothes. I gather everything up and go back to the closet. Open the doors. Turn on the lights. Shove the clothes in the appropriate hampers. Delicates. Dry Cleaning. Putting on some clean black lace panties – my favorite color for undies, I look around for something to wear. I'm not wearing my masturbation clothing due to some out-of-this-world feeling that Alex would know what I did if I wore them. I had a feeling that my nipples were going to tighten up the next time I saw Alex—traitors that they are. They would be determined to give me away. Then I see it. A blousy dress I had when I wanted my shape to be formless. This house dress – or moo-moo as the tag said when I bought it - was great to relax around the house in. When I wear that, there is no figure or breasts to attract notice. It is better than a potato sack. And let's face it, my nipples are still tender from all my groping. Just might have over did it – but *D-A-M-N!* Alex is great masturbation candy. I put on the housedress, turn out the closet lights and close the door. As I walk to the bedroom door, I am feeling lighter. Happier. Like I have taken a brief vacation. My tummy rumbles so I head for the kitchen. I wonder if Alex likes fajitas.

Chapter 7

I have the homemade fajita tortillas sitting on the butcher block alongside the bowl of four-color types of bell peppers and white onions that I have already cooked. I get in a mood every so often and make batches of homemade tortillas of flour or corn and seal them in airless containers for occasions when I get in the mood for them. This way it was easy to whip up a quick Mexican meal and still have homemade. Chicken and steak are each frying in separate skillets when Alex suddenly enters and stops.

"Hi," I greet him with an overly friendly voice because I'm nervous. *Am I blushing?* I'm feeling guilty about what I had done with him as my co-star. "Hungry?" I ask him. God knows I am.

"Yeah, I could eat," he smiles and sets his satchel down. I wonder if he has a toolbelt in there. I have always had a fantasy of a workman fucking me on a kitchen counter. I bet all women do. He goes to the sink with one of those tall, stainless steel coffee mugs and begins rinsing it out. I imagine he'd had it filled with coffee and had finished it all.

It is then I remember that I had NOT turned off the camera in my master bedroom. I freeze. Maybe fantasizing about him watching me was actually my sixth sense letting me know that he really was.

"Are you all finished?" I ask as I turn to him, hoping my face isn't giving away the moon.

"No. I'll do the cameras next and be out of your hair in no time." He responds, causing me to relax. I did notice he left his mug upside down in the sink before taking one of the stools in front of the butcher block kitchen island I am working at.

"No hurries. You've been working for quite a while. Relax. Want a beer?" I'm nervous, and it is showing, at least to me, in my chatty attitude.

"Yeah, a beer sounds great. But I thought you didn't have anything unhealthy in here?" He smiles as he asks.

God, that smile could take me to the moon and back!

I go to the Sub-Zero fridge and bring back two cold bottles and hand one to him. "I only buy organic beer. Hope that's okay," I smile as I twist off my cap.

"Fine by me," he grins as he twists off his own cap and scans the label. I know it will go down cold and delicious for him. It is a special craft beer that I had stumbled across and not only bought several dozen bottles after tasting it but invested in the company as well. We are prepping to go regional and then national. I set my bottle on the island in front of me.

"Fajitas okay?" I ask as I continue with my cooking.

"Love 'em. Mexican food and beer. You trying to wrangle a cheaper bill out of me?"

I laugh out loud. *The bill has nothing to do with anything*, I thought to myself. *Is the way to a man's cock through his stomach?*

It isn't long before we are both perched on the stools enjoying our homemade fajitas, guacamole, and salsa. The sour cream is the only thing that came from the store, but it's out of a glass container, and it's organic. I bragged to Alex that I had made the tortillas myself. I chatted about the cooking class I had taken a few years back. I had been going through a bored streak, and that had helped spice things up considerably, both literally and figuratively. For a while. *Nothing compared to the way Alex could spice me up.*

"So, what do you do for a living? If you don't mind my asking?" he asks as he makes his third helping of fajitas, combining the steak and chicken together. I love watching him eat. And, of course, I want him to eat me with those strong, white, perfect teeth of his.

"I'm a novelist," I hear myself say, still imagining his lips between my legs.

"And a very good one by the looks of this place," he intones.

"I got lucky. I do a series about female vampires, and it's big with the women." I don't tell him – or anyone else, for that matter - that a movie company has bought my first five books in the series for a staggering price, and that was the reason I could afford this house. Nobody needs to know how much money I have.

"What? No male vamps?" he teases before taking another bite of his already almost-gone fajitas, and he looks to be contemplating a fourth.

"They think they're all gone," I say. "So, they have to get with human men."

"And do they mind 'getting' with human men?" he asks with a teasing look in his eyes.

"They make do," I smile.

"Ouch!" He fakes an arrow, taking out his heart, which causes me to laugh again. "I feel as if I should defend my sex somehow."

"Help me clean up the kitchen, and we'll call it even," I'm only half kidding.

"You're on!" He pledges as we both keep eating.

Chapter 8

We are done cleaning up the kitchen, one of two dishwashers is running, and I am drying my hands. It seems like my opportunity to keep him near me is fading. He said he had to go finish the cameras and once he did, he'd be totally done. When would I be alone with him again? It is now or never.

"So," I begin as I hang up the kitchen towel on a rack at the side of the kitchen island. "You have a toolbelt in that satchel?"

"Yeah, I use one sometimes when I have to climb poles or need more than one tool and there's not always a table or platform to lay my tools on."

"Can I see it?"

Shrugging, he leans down and brings his satchel onto the kitchen island. He flips the flap over and unzips it. It is the work of a moment for him to pull it out and hold it up for me.

"No, I mean, can I see you with it on?"

He puts the belt on and holds his hands up to show me.

"Well, don't you have to have tools in it for it to be a toolbelt?" I cross my arms in front of my chest to cover my nervousness, and I give him a look that I hope says, "Duh." If this is getting weird for him, he doesn't show it as he fills the belt with the tools and moves out from behind the island so he is facing me.

"Take off your shirt," I command breathlessly.

Instantly, he whips off his shirt, drops it to the floor, and just waits, panting.

"Your boots next."

The boots come off.

"Do I have to tell you the rest?"

"Yes," he replies, "I want you to tell me everything you want."

My heart is POUNDING. My hands are sweating. My breasts and nipples tingling. And I instantly get wet between my legs.

"I want you to make love to me on this kitchen island."

My. Fantasy. Realized.

He has his clothes off in a heartbeat. Just the toolbelt stays on. He has me up onto my kitchen island before my next breath. My housedress is next. He is kissing me. But not the full-open-mouth swallow your face, tongue-thrusting down your throat that chokes you. He actually kisses my lips. I have automatically opened my mouth, but he stays on my lips. Kissing them. Gently sucking on them. Occasionally biting them gently. Even the corners of my mouth get loving attention. Even the licking he does is selective. Directive.

I have tried to reach between us and grab that magnificent cock that I had seen all too briefly as he had approached me. But he uses his big shoulders and arms to deter me. I am getting frustrated. And then it hits me. This is no ordinary lover. No slam-bam-thank-you-ma'am lothario. All the times me and my girlfriends have bitched that men don't take their time and never worry about our pleasure. And now that I have it, I have just fallen into the routine rut of trying to hurry to the end.

Lay back and enjoy it! I admonish myself.

Then he Frenches me. I suck his tongue in. I can't help myself. All the attention he has paid to kissing me, and I am ready for something in my mouth. His tongue. His cock. I am so ready.

His hands play with my hair, stroking it, running his fingers through it. Then he's at my shoulders, massaging them as we keep up the French kissing. Then he holds my neck. You know how you see that in the movies, but men never do it. He does it, and it turns me on so much, it shocks me. Then he is kissing my face all over. Unhurried.

Gently. Deliberately. Then his teeth are on my earlobes, and he pulls gently and releases them as they slide through his teeth.

My. Clit. Weeps.

"God damn it! Suck my tits!" I moaned out of control as my head lulls back.

"No," he teases.

The lips between my thighs throb at his disobedience.

He nibbles my throat and collarbones. Now, I am practically lying across the cutting board part of the island; only his arms along my back are keeping me up.

Finally! Finally! Finally, he arches my back up and puts my breasts right in his face, nuzzling them. *Major G-spot, dude*, and my moaning is low and continuous like a purring cat, so he must know it. He gently takes the first one in his lips and tongues the tip.

Fuck me! Fuck me! Fuck me! Echoes through my brain as I start writhing and moaning louder. Teasing my breasts with his teeth drives me even more crazy and then he sucks.

I. Climax. Hard.

He must have laid me on the countertop and moved his arms out to the side, leaning on them while he watched me. I had no idea at the time it was happening. I was off in the ether of pleasure, panting, my eyes closed. Shutters were going through my body. But when I opened my eyes, I saw that my hands were on his biceps, holding on for dear life as if anchoring myself to the earth because he had sent me so high. I loosened my grip and then gently squeezed both of his biceps at the same time as sort of a 'thank you.' It seems to take a while for my brain to come back online. I focus on his face.

"Thank you," I murmur.

"My pleasure," he whispers with a smile.

"No, I mean, thank you for letting me enjoy it instead of insisting on getting inside me immediately. I've never had a man do that for me before."

"Again, my pleasure," he whispers and gently kisses my lips.

"Now I need you to fuck me hard. Not that I didn't love what you just did, but I don't want you to die from blue balls, and I need to feel you inside me."

He throws back his head and laughs, and I take that opportunity to grab his cock. He almost jack-knifes back into the sink. I use both of my hands on his cock to pull him back to me. Now he is the one panting and moaning. His cock is hard and beautiful. He pushes me back down, frees his cock from my grip, and spreads my legs wide. He slams into me. I was more than ready and no longer had a cervix to hit, so I'm good with the pummeling. We both shout out loud. He grabs my hips and pulls me forward as he slams into meet me. I wrap my legs around his hard, tight ass. My back is supported by the counter, and I throw my arms up to the edge of the butcher block as I try to keep myself stabilized. My breasts are flapping back and forth with each punch of his hips, and it's turning me on more. He jackhammers into me as his hot liquid fills me up until it's running out of me. At least no one was going to have to lay in the wet spot. The counter was an easy cleanup.

I get off again and he can't seem to stop. He finally does and he leans in against me and puts his arms back on the counter to support himself. He is panting like a racehorse, and I feel very self-satisfied as I smile at him.

"Let's do that again," I purr.

"Your wish, my command." He throws me up over his broad shoulder as he strides off toward what I hoped was going to be my bedroom. Having a soft surface to navigate on was what we needed. I shriek in surprise and begin giggling like a girl. Like a girl! I reach down and swat his ass, and his head turns, and he gently bites my ass.

"Left! Left!" I cry out as he takes a wrong turn, and we are soon in my bedroom. He kicks - kicks! - the door shut like he's Tarzan or something and tosses me onto the bed. As I bounce, I laugh and open my arms to him. He is so magnificent, all Chris Hemsworth – only better—because Alex's actually here. He climbs into the bed and into my arms and starts stroking my skin.

"Please tell me – now that some sanity has returned – that there is no husband that's going to be bursting through the bedroom door at any moment," he grins, but the look on his face says he is only half kidding.

"That would be awkward," I laughed. "But, no, no husband or boyfriend. Not even a frenetic fan has been stalking me."

"Now, that, I find hard to believe, considering how many crazy people there are out there in L.A." He responds as we both laugh and begin kissing again. This time I am taking control, and I grab hold of his cock quickly and roll him to his back as I loom over him. I am hoping there will be time later for slow lovemaking again, but right now, I have to have him. I settle between his legs, stroking his cock and balls. I love looking at him, and he lets my hands explore every inch of him. And trust me, there is a lot to explore. I slide down between his legs and put my mouth on his balls, slowly sucking one in and playing with it with my tongue. Then I pop that one out, pulling as I go, and his eyes roll into the back of his head. I sucked the next one in and did the same thing. His cock was perfect. Pink and purple and standing tall like it was made of steel. But the skin around it is warm and soft.

I start licking the head of his cock, swirling my tongue around and brushing through the crease at the top of his head, knowing he will love it. Then I double-hand his shaft and gently began twisting opposite of each other as I stroked up and down.

"F-u-c-k!" he breathes. His cock starts coming. I suck him in my mouth and swallow every drop. When he becomes too sensitive, I ease away. This time I get to watch him. He seems boneless. I wait until his eyes look at me, and I lick my lips. He gathers me into his arms, and we hold each other. It is quiet for a long time.

"So, should we call it a night?" I ask as I look up at him. This had been the longest sex session I'd had, so I figured I'd better be realistic about it.

"Never!" he whispers. Rolling on top of me, he begins kissing me again like he had in the kitchen. I am all in for doing another long, slow session, except it doesn't take long for my moans to fill the room and his join mine because this time, he doesn't keep me away from his cock. Soon he is kissing his way to my breasts, and he takes my nipples between his fingers. He gently rolls them back and forth as he licks up my sternum and softly nips at my breasts.

Was that a fire alarm ringing? Because I was in desperate need for my flames to be put out. My legs begin sawing, and he insists on spending some time kissing my belly button as his hands gently knead my breasts.

Finally, he lifts my legs over his back and settles his face between my thighs, so his mouth is close to my weeping slit. Just knowing he is there hikes up my excitement, and my moans must tell him he is driving me crazy. He takes one long lick up my clit from bottom to top.

"Oh, God!" I gasp loudly. He does it again. And again. And soon, he is eating me. Reaching up with one hand, he encircles my leg and comes down from the top of my sex and uses two fingers to spread my swollen lower lips wide. And while he continued to tongue me, his other hand came up from under me, and he slid two fingers into my hot wet slit and finger fucks me.

I AM SCREAMING HIS NAME OVER AND OVER!

It is like I am coming but not coming. Like I can't reach the apex. I want to cry; it feels so good, but I can't get THERE! Suddenly, I feel his thumb slide into my ass. A guttural scream gasps out of me. I've never been interested in anyone ever putting anything near my ass, but *D-A-M-N!* My explosion must have topped Mount St. Helen's. It is the most pleasurable experience of my life.

And then it happens. I start to cry for real.

He removes his fingers and takes me into his arms, pulling the comforter up from the bottom of the bed and putting it over both of us. He doesn't say anything. I feel so vulnerable. I didn't even want to open my eyes to look at him because the little shutters and sparks were still coming.

Chapter 9

Morning. I open my eyes. Yes, it is morning. I turn my head quickly to look at Alex, but he is gone. Maybe. Just maybe he is in the kitchen. I get up and go to the closet. The door opens automatically. The lights come on. That's right, I remind myself. He had been here to service the house, not just me. I throw on one of my sexy, black lace robes that can easily be removed and head out as I tie the belt. All the doors open and close for me. The curtains are open where they were supposed to be open. I can smell the coffee all the way from the kitchen. Everything looks as if it is running properly. His work is done; is he gone now?

Ringing.

My phone. Where was my cell phone? I feel disoriented in my own home. My office. I hurry there and move the papers around until I find it.

"Yeah?" I answer abruptly.

"Well, it doesn't sound like you got laid at all!"

"Hello, Sylvia. I was in the middle of something; sorry if I sounded so gruff."

"Well, it couldn't possibly be sex, or you wouldn't have answered at all. At least, I hope not! Not even you are that cold."

"Thanks for the validation, Sylvia," I remark dryly as I head out of my office toward the kitchen.

"So, are you going to tell me what happened with Mister Alex McCall, or are you going to make me beg?"

"I think I'll make you beg; you do it so well," I tease as I take a quick look in the kitchen but find it empty. Empty. *God damn it*! My mood takes a quick dive into Hell as I slowly walk into my living room and go over to the floor-to-ceiling fish tank and look at the fish. "Listen, Sylvia, can I call you back? I'm in the middle of something – writing – you know."

"Sure, sweetie. You, okay?" she sounded worried.

"Yeah, gotta deadline. You know. Later," I say and hit the 'end call' button. I let the iPhone slip from my fingers, and it hits the carpet. I slowly walk to the electronics room, not having a hope that he will be there. And he isn't. I wander aimlessly around the house, occasionally perching on a sofa or a chair, pull my legs up, and wrap my arms around them as if to comfort myself. I don't know what I am all down in the dumps about. We didn't make any plans. We'd both gotten laid. I had control of my house back, and he was getting paid. Hell, I should probably tip him for the great sex. He's a young guy; why in the hell would I think he'd want to stay hooked up to an old lady? Yeah, I keep myself looking good, but let's face it, I am at least twenty years older than he is. *Old enough to be his mother, for Christ's sake.* Yeah, I'm sure he'd like to take Mom out to parties with him.

I finally return to my bedroom and go into the closet, the doors and lights doing their jobs. I remove the robe because I feel stupid staying in it. I get into a sweatshirt and sweatpants without any underwear. My body is still on a live wire circuit from the sex, and I don't want anything rubbing up against me. I climb onto my still unmade bed with the slightly rumpled covers and pull the comforter over me. I know I am going to take a depression nap. I always have one wash over me whenever I go through such a big disappointment.

The gate bell rings.

My eyes pop open. Have I slept? I think I have. I look over at the bedside monitor. A man, sitting on a Harley in a dark helmet and leathers, is waving at the monitor.

"What do you want?" I ask as soon as I hit the call button on the monitor. "All you have to do is bill my credit card."

It is as if he goes rock-solid still. Then he slowly opens his visor. His blue eyes reach me right through the monitor.

"So, was this just a get-fucked-by-the-hired-help fantasy, and now you're done with me?" he said with the same dry manner I use on other people.

"I'm not the one who left without a word," I snap.

"I left you a note," he offered.

"Where?" I asked, my breath catching.

"By the coffee pot. I figured that would be your first stop when you got up."

I RUN TO THE KITCHEN.

Sure enough, right where he said it would be. Beautifully written in actual cursive writing. Gym. Shower. Appointment. Back with dinner. Of course, he had used actual full sentences, but I only noticed the bullet points at this moment. Hurrying to the monitor in the kitchen, I hit the gate release and re-read the note more slowly. At the sound of the Harley pulling up to the front door, I rushed down to it. Throwing the door wide with the button, I jump over the transom like I'm jumping onto a swimming pool. Alex had removed his helmet and was dismounting the bike. I ran over and jumped into his arms, and we kissed softly but intently for a while. When we both came up for air, he asked –

"Do you like Italian?"

"Why, are you Italian?" I asked with a grin.

"Dinner," he grinned back.

"Can't we fuck first?" I ask hopefully.

"Dinner will get cold"

"That's what ovens are for," I inform him with as sexy a look as I can muster.

"Well, then, that sounds like a plan," he says, hoisting me up higher, grabbing the bags of food out of his saddlebags, and heading into the house.

The doors close on their own.

—The End—

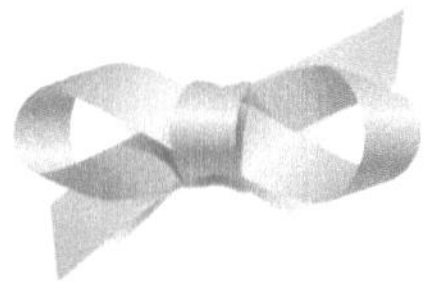

BONUS

HUNKY NERD 2: CHLOE & DAEVON

Chloe walked inside the elevator as soon as the doors opened. Pushing the button for the sixteenth floor, she glanced up at the numbers above the doors and watched, out of habit, as they ran down.

Here in the Winston Towers, every possible desire was catered to - well, almost. Let's just say the legal ones were. They had butlers, maids, valets, chefs, and even a team of concierges in the lobby. The first floor was filled with restaurants, gift shops, jewelry stores, and a grocery. The rest - excluding level sixteen - all the way to the twenty-fourth floor were luxury residential apartments. You could cook your own meals, have your butler do it, order from a downstairs restaurant and have it delivered, or go to the ground floor and pick your own restaurant. Hell's bells, a concierge would even go to Taco Bell for you.

She dropped her eyes to the mirrored walls of the elevator and inspected her image. Yep, she was all that and a bag of chips, as a stranger on the street had recently exclaimed. Her body was slamming. Her cocoa skin flawless, her waist small, her belly flat, her ass perfect and her breasts were round, high, and tight.

And why not?

She worked hard at it which was exactly why she was headed for the gym on the sixteenth floor. Well, actually, the gym WAS the entire sixteenth floor. With every possible exercise machine; weight bench; hand weights, bar bells, rope tug - whip - push me, pull you - there wasn't any part of your body that couldn't be built up or slimmed down. There were even two swimming pools. Both hung off either side of the building. One with lanes for laps swimmers and one for everybody else. You just couldn't be afraid of heights because the pools were see-through. Sixteen floors to the street. And while Chloe got lots of attention - even from the dedicated body builders - she was already familiar with most of the men who used the gym and there wasn't really anything she was interested in.

With a loud ding, the mirrored doors of the elevator parted, revealing a busy gym. Chloe strode in like she owned the place, which was pretty much how she lived her life. She was a young woman who owned and ran her own highly successful cosmetic company that catered to women of color, a group that the regular cosmetic companies typically overlooked or only paid lip service to. Chloe had become a chemist in college with developing her own cosmetics in mind. While still in school she had created a foundation that went on clear and then took on the exact shade of the wearer and created a flawless coverage that fit every skin type - even white skin. She had followed that with lipsticks that lasted overnight and never dried out the lips. Her Lip Line had absolutely every possible color, even a couple that had been deemed impossible. She had graduated summa cum laude by the time she made her first million bucks.

Chloe stopped suddenly. She could almost hear the sound of a scratching record inside her head as if the stylist had been knocked out of the grooves to skip along the record. Or was that screeching tires?

There, on a weight bench pressing more pounds than what seemed humanly possible, was one fucking fine man. His dark chocolate skin was smooth and hairless. He was in a tank top and shorts. His legs were sculpted with perfect muscle as were his arms and chest. He wasn't bulky like a bodybuilder.

No. He-was-perfect.

As Chloe watched those massive arms go up and down like well-oiled machines, her nipples began to tingle, and she couldn't help but rub her thighs together slightly. She wanted to do it a little more aggressively. However, other eyes were upon her, and she didn't want to be obvious about her reaction to that beautiful, glorious man who had yet to look at her. He was completely involved with what he was doing.

Well, time was a-wastin'. He just needed to get on the Chloe train right now! That man didn't realize what he was missing, and it was up to her to educate him now. Not now - NOW!

Chloe noticed there was a free weight on the floor next to where he was working out. His spotter was a guy Chloe had seen at the gym before. Jimmy-Johnny or Joey - whatever. He had even chatted her up a couple of times, but he wasn't her type. No, her type was lying on his back with his legs spread, his feet on the floor to counterbalance all that metal he was lifting over his head. Chloe knew exactly what to do. She casually moved around to the other side of the weight bench Mister Perfect was on and stood over what looked to be just a five-pound free weight someone had left on the floor. Certainly, Mister Arms, who put Schwarzenegger to shame, hadn't been using it before he started pumping the massive stuff. Standing in front of the free weight, her back to Mister-about-to-cover-her-with-his-massive form, Chloe put her feet together and S-L-O-W-L-Y bent down from the waist as if she were going to pick up the free weight, showing Mister Hot Melting Butter what she knew was a wonderful view of her ass and her cleft in her tight yoga pants.

Daevon felt the tremor. Someone had entered the gym that sent invisible waves of power that disturbed, well, okay - the Force. Someone secure and self-possessed was moving through the gym as if to take over. His cock thickened up. Either in aggression or for possession, it just depended on the sex of that mini quake moving through the room. It wasn't long before he knew it was a female. She had moved next to him and was bending down for something on the floor. He wasn't made of stone. He had to divert his eyes from the weight bar to that perfectly formed ass. His mouth watered.

D-A-M-N! he thought to himself, and he quickly got his attention back to the three-hundred-fifty pounds he was pushing before it got out of his control and took out his chest. He returned the load to the supports, and his spotter, James, helped him get it home.

Chloe returned upright with the weight in her hand and walked it over to the line of free weights and returned it to an empty place. She used the mirrored wall in front of herself to see what Man-Of-Her-Dreams was doing. Well, damn it, she thought to herself; he was lying there with a gym towel on his face, his hands holding it in place as if he was resting. Don't tell her that she had wasted her best stretch for nothing. The spotter grinned at her in appreciation, but she wasn't after his notice. Turning her nose up, Chloe went to the treadmill that she always started with, set the controls to her workout, and began walking.

As Daevon removed the towel from his face and sat up, he was very aware that his cock had expanded to fill the front of his workout shorts. If he stood up now, he'd have some major tent action going on that no one in the gym would fail to notice. He used his peripheral vision to check out that beautiful woman who had got him into this condition. She was on the treadmill, those long, lovely legs clad tightly in yoga pants along with that great ass. He suddenly had an image of her on all fours as he used her hips for support and piston his cock in and out of her swollen pussy as if he were setting a new land speed record.

He groaned.

"Yeah, she's something all right," James intoned with a big grin on his face. "You thinking of fucking that?"

"Crude, dude," Daevon muttered as he wiped his neck with the towel.

"Hey, don't be pretending with me. You're the one with the baseball bat in your shorts," James finished with a small laugh. Daevon threw a glare at his buddy before dropping the towel in his lap for some additional coverage. He closed his eyes and concentrated on his recovery breathing, hoping it calmed his Mister Baseball bat down enough for him to move on through the rest of his workout.

Chloe was irritated beyond belief. What was wrong with that man? She had glanced from the overhead television screens to the mirrored wall to see if he was watching her. He wasn't! His eyes were closed, his hands on his hips and he was breathing long and slow as if he was recovering from his workout. He didn't know what a workout was if he'd never had sex with her! This was just too much. She never had to work so hard to get someone's attention before. She decided two could play that game, so she upped her workout stress on the treadmill and started running. After all, she was here to get through her workout before she had to go to her company. She was just going to put that man out of her mind. Besides, he was probably gay which would certainly explain why he was resistant to her. But even gay men had appreciated her before. This man probably knew how delicious he was and was playing hard to get. Well, Chloe would just see who would get whom.

How Daevon got through his workout, he was unsure. Now, as he stood in the gym's locker room shower, he let the water rain into his face while he finally allowed himself to think of that beautiful woman who had barged into his brain and refused to get out. As he soaped himself up in his lone, curtained cubical, his touch activated his cock with all the soapy ministration. And he hadn't even touched himself there yet! He finally reached down and snagged his cock like it was a wild stallion trying to buck away.

"Oh, fuck!" he barked out as he took ahold of himself and began to pump. His other hand locked around his large sac, and he played, pulled, and squeezed himself as he drove himself to a quick orgasm with his tight fist plunging up and down on his steel cock. Cum shot out of him as if it were barking out its own curses. He leaned his hot cheek against the shower tile and rested, making himself deliberately release his cock and balls, which were vibrating like they'd been hit by lightning. Damn, he thought. If just thinking about her did this to him, what would the actual thing be like?

Chloe pulled off her sweaty gym clothes. She put them in a plastic bag with her I.D. number on it and plopped them into the gym laundry chute so they could be cleaned and returned to her apartment. That man was on her last nerve, and she was done with him. He wasn't going to occupy her mind anymore. She was done with Mister I'm-so-big-bad-and-beautiful-I'm-too-good-to-look-at-Chloe! She grabbed up her shower items, walked into the shower stall, and snapped that goddamned plastic curtain into place. And it better stay there if it knew what was good for it. Hanging her netted bag on the hook away from where the spray would be hitting, she turned to the water valves and twisted them on. She stood to the side of the spray until she got it adjusted. And her netted bag, filled with her shampoo, conditioner, and body wash - made by her company, of course - was indeed out of the spray.

Chloe stepped under the spray and just stood there as the water cascaded down her head, face, breasts, and curves, past her belly, and streamed down her long legs. Leaning her head down, she let the spray nail her neck. Blindly reaching out, she carefully adjusted the water a little hotter, and when it was just right, a deep sigh escaped from her lips. She had worked out even harder than necessary because she was mad as hell at that chocolate caramel candy man. Boom! There she was, thinking about him again. Damn it! She turned her face up to the spray

She had managed to get through her shampooing and was now applying her conditioner before she thought of him again. Reaching into the netted bag to put the conditioner back in, she had some time to wait while the conditioner did its thing. She took out her scrubber and face products. As she worked in the cleaner with the soft-bristle scrubber, her mind began to drift. The cleaner went back into the bag, but she didn't remember doing it. The circular scrubber left her face and went to her neck, over each shoulder, and down to her left breast. She wound up concentrating on the nipple. The vibration and the tender, soft bristles sent electrical waves throughout her body until she was aching between her legs. She switched it to the right breast, going around and around until she was at her other nipple. Again, she spent time there, her whole body tuning up that ache. Soon her free hand was rubbing her left breast while the circulating brush teased the right nipple. Before long, the scrubber had been returned to the bag, and both her hands were running all over her body. But in her mind - it was his hands. His broad palms cupping her large round breasts. Pinching her nipples just right. Pulling them slightly. None of this dialing an old-fashioned radio tuner, like she was a video game that needed to be cranked, yanked, and pulled. But gently. Softly. Smoothly. Chloe was panting now. Her hands both ran down to her belly and caressed it. Out to her hips. Kneading them. Smoothing them. Around to her ass. Grabbing it. Massaging it. Moving around to that special place between her legs. Her pussy was throbbing with anticipation. She was warmly wet and not from the shower. Her fingers of her left hand spread her pussy lips, and her right hand slid two long fingers in deep. Chloe groaned. Her eyes were closed, and she was seeing him between her legs. It was his fingers spreading her for his use. His tongue, instead of her fingers, licked deep inside her. Chloe let herself fall back against the wall, her head meeting her netted bag. She quickly moved over until just the wall was holding her up. She lifted her leg and rested her foot on a built-in soap holder. Her fingers - or rather, his tongue - were able to access more of her engorged pussy, which was already on the verge of coming. She stopped everything and held still; her eyes still closed. She didn't want to cum just yet. She wanted to draw it out. Make it last.

When she thought she was in control again, she began moving her fingers - his tongue again. She released, holding open her pussy, and let her left hand - his hand smooth its way back up to her breast and gently squeeze and roll her nipple. His fingers - tongue - whatever the fuck

- started moving faster and faster inside her. The wet smacking sound rising above the sound of the shower.

Chloe cried out as she exploded in a glorious climax. She was drifting in the clouds. But she was also breathing like a racehorse that just finished Church Hill Downs. The vibration slowing down and down and down. She was finally level when she opened her eyes. It was then she realized she'd done this in a very public place.

Fuck.

She finished her hair and shower, taking extra time so that any spectators that might have heard anything got bored and left instead of hanging out to see who had pleasured herself in such an exuberant way. She turned off her shower and spent some time drying off with the two towels she had previously hung over the shower rod. When she quietly parted the curtains, she glanced around and there was no one in the immediate area. Her hair and body were each wrapped in their own towels, and she took her things to her locker. Some women came in, looking sweaty like they had just finished their workout too. She took her grooming items to the mirrors over the sinks. There was no one in there. Maybe she had lucked out and no one had been privy to her pleasuring. But they could be sitting out at the juice bar waiting for her to emerge. If that was the case, she'd take her time.

So, she groomed herself until she looked like a million bucks.

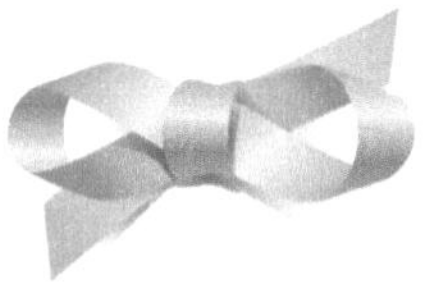

CHAPTER TWO: CHLOE & DAEVON

Daevon was enjoying a glass of red wine as his dinner plate was delivered. A big, juicy steak, a large baked yam with real butter, steamed asparagus spears, and no bread. His salad in a side bowl, just the way he liked it. With lemon juice, virgin olive oil, and apple cider vinegar for his dressing. Not served ahead of his meal but at the same time. He liked everything at once so he could decide what he wanted to put in his mouth and when. He couldn't do that if it were served in separate courses.

He said his thanks to his waiter and lifted his wine up for another drink. Over the round body of his wine glass, he saw that incredible woman from the gym walk into the steak house. Chloe. That was her name. His weight trainer had been very forthcoming with everything he knew about the woman. She had developed her own make-up line which had made her a great deal of money. She was single. Lived in the building up on the twenty-fourth floor, which meant half of that floor belonged to her. There were only two penthouses and she owned one. Her eyes scanned the room and landed on him. As if he heard some silent call, he rose from his chair and moved to the empty chair near his and pulled it out, looking at her, smiling all the while.

Chloe had managed to get through her day - somehow - without thinking about the gorgeous bastard from the gym. She loved her company and micro-managed every division without micromanaging it. She had hired all the best people, but they had to keep her up-date-on-everything by walking her through everything. They had to show her too. And Chloe never let an opportunity pass by without asking her techs what their opinions were about the procedures being run. Often finding better ways of tweaking things from the people in the trenches who were doing the work. She encouraged individuality and didn't tolerate bullies. She wanted her company to be a safe place to work. There was only one boss, however, and that was her. And usually, that was all she needed to focus on. But that man had been a challenge.

Despite throwing herself into the matters of the day, she felt very hungry, and the salad she'd had at lunch hadn't been enough. She needed meat.

A. Great. Big. Piece. Of. Meat.

And since she didn't get to play on the jungle gym, she'd had her eye on, she'd have to go the steakhouse. Indulging in a piece of meat cooked to her specs seemed all she could do. At first, she thought of inviting someone from work. Or maybe one of her girlfriends. But she was having a hard enough time concentrating and didn't want her guests to feel like she was ignoring them.

After being welcomed into the steakhouse, she let her eyes skim the room while the Host gathered a menu for her.

There. He. Was.

Sitting alone at a table. His meal was already in front of him. A wine glass at his lips. As she followed the host, that tall, gorgeous, black man smiled at her and rose from his seat. He pulled out the chair next to him as though he had expected her. Her nipples tingled, and she got wet between her legs. Her lips parted so she could breathe a little easier.

Just who did he think he was? she wondered as she tossed her head and followed the host to her own table. Big, Bad, and Beautiful wasn't going to smile at her and crook his little finger, and she'd come running. If anybody came running, it was going to be him - to her!

If she expected him to look disappointed, he wasn't. He just kept on smiling pleasantly, pushed in the still vacant chair, and reseated himself in front of his meal. He dug in as if that meat was the best thing he'd ever eaten, making her jealous of his meal.

The host seated her in a semi-circular booth by pulling out the table and allowing her to sit before he slid it back in toward her. He handed her the menu.

"Tell me, Jamal," Chloe began quietly, pretending to look at the menu.

"Yes, Miss Roberts?" he asked just as quietly.

"Without turning around, would you know whom I'd be asking about if I said he was a very tall, well-built black male dining alone?"

"Yes, Miss. That would be Mister Daevon Singleton. Owns his own electronics corporation. Works with the government, I believe. Single. No children. No females in and out that I've been made aware of."

"Is he straight? she gave a little half laugh.

"Unfortunately, yes." Jamal replied. Chloe shot him a look, and he gave her a professional smile.

"So, what's he having?"

"Medium rare rib eye steak, baked yam with butter, steamed asparagus, and a side salad with lemon, virgin olive oil, and apple cider vinegar for dressing."

"Apple cider vinegar?"

"Yes, Miss."

Chloe mulled that over.

"I'll have what he's having; hold the yam and bring everything else on the same plate."

"Yes, Miss," acknowledged Jamal. "Would Miss like the steak cut in half and saved for your dog, Midas?" he inquired.

"You know me so well, Jamal, yes please."

"Wine?" Jamal inquired.

"What he's having," they both said at the same time.

Daevon was able to enjoy his dinner by pretending he was eating her. She was sitting across the room all cool and collected. Looking at her iPhone. He knew he was driving her crazy because she was doing the same to him. Whatever heat that was between them just couldn't be ignored - not if your heart was beating and you were still breathing. The only thing that was going to get in their way was pride. Someone was going to have to give if this was ever going to come to fruition.

Chloe had to admit that the apple cider vinegar did add a zip to the salad. She had always used wine vinegar or balsamic. But this was a nice change. She was just about finished. Her doggie bag for Midas was on its way to her dog walker, Kevin, who babysat her Great Dane whenever she was working or away. The wonderful wine - of which, uncharacteristically, she'd had two glasses - was making her feel reckless.

Daevon slid in beside her.

"Hello. We haven't been properly introduced yet. I'm Daevon Singleton," he said as he offered that big hand to her. She took it and shook it back. Her hand was completely lost inside of his. But what was not lost was that instant heat. They both felt it.

"Chloe Roberts."

They held hands just a little too long as if they were both savoring that electrical thrill between them.

"I thought we could have dessert," he smiled gleamingly as he let go of her hand.

"I don't eat dessert, thank you."

She missed his touch already.

Daevon put his left arm up on the back side of the booth behind her and his right arm on the table in front of himself so he could turn his body to face hers.

"But this dessert burns calories instead of adding them."

She arched a brow at him.

"Are you saying we should go someplace and have sex? Please, you're an absolute stranger." Her heart pounded as her brain screamed, yes, yes, fuck me! Fuck me!

"Afraid to be alone with me?"

Chloe thought about that. When she had first laid eyes on him, there had been this instant lust. She hadn't worried about it then. And now that he was so close, she realized how big he was, but she still wanted him. Still.

"We can do it right here."

Chloe's mouth dropped open in astonishment.

"You are insane! You're just going to throw me atop this table and ravish me in front of God and everyone. Besides asking us to leave the restaurant, I'm sure the management of the building would throw me out of my penthouse and you out of whatever floor you live on!"

He chuckled softly with that Barry-White-deep voice and whispered: "It will be all about you. Ever want to do something naughty in public, and those around you don't know about it?

She went wet between her legs, her pussy raising its hand, screaming I want me some of that! "What did you have in mind," she whispered breathlessly.

The waiter showed up just at that moment to clear her plate.

"Is there anything else I can get either of you?"

"Yes," Daevon began, "the lady isn't interested in dessert, but I will have the chocolate mousse, please."

"No wonder you have to work out so hard," Chloe began as the waiter left. "Do you know how much sugar is in that chocolate mousse?"

"Dessert has to be sweet if it's going to compete with you"

"Ha!" she laughed, "Please!"

"What I'm going to do," he began whispering in that voice, "is run my hand up into your pussy to pleasure you while I eat that mousse, pretending all the while that I'm eating you."

Her pussy pounded with a heartbeat of its own.

Her breasts now raised their hands! Chloe tried to speak but couldn't because he had pulled his left arm from behind her and put his hot hand under the table until it was on her knee. What she really going to let him do this? In such a public place?

Yes, please, the rest of her body weighed in with the opinion poll. She knew the tablecloth would hide anything that went on under the table, but she didn't know how he was going to Houdini his hand around to be able to reach up her skirt.

The chocolate mousse arrived.

Daevon pulled the tall fountain glass toward him as he turned his body back to the table and picked up the long spoon. He licked the spoon before he even had it dessert on it. He sucked on the spoon slowly. Then used his tongue to trace the outline of the spoon. Chloe couldn't take her eyes off him as his hand gently rubbed her leg, slowly moving up, her skirt offering no barrier.

He dipped the spoon into the creamy dessert and brought it to his mouth. His tongue teased the chocolatey treat as his fingers found her silk panties and began massaging her clit through them. Her legs automatically spread wider for his convenience as she watched him tongue that dessert. Soon his fingers had pushed aside her panties and plunged into her wet lips, massaging and teasing.

It was everything Chloe could do to keep her breathing normal. She wanted to groan. She wanted to moan. She wanted his tongue to do to her what it was doing to that dessert. His fingers probed deeper, taking up a pulling, plunging sensation that was driving her wild. He was right. Knowing he was doing this to her in a public place really cranked up the sensations. She looked around to see if anyone was looking. Noticing. Suspecting.

No one was.

Her breasts were on fire, screaming for attention. To keep her from fondling herself, she slid her fingers through the crease at the back of the booth and grabbed a hold. Without realizing it, she hiked her right knee over one of his to spread herself wider and leaned back against the booth. His talented hand took full advantage of all the room she granted him. And he continued to make love to that silky, moist dessert. She wanted to rock her hips but was afraid that would draw attention. The wet sound of those broad fingers fucking her seemed loud to her own ears and she looked at him. He smiled as his lips sucked in that chocolate.

She came hard.

Her eyes had clamped shut as she exploded and suddenly his lips were on hers and he was kissing her thoroughly. She tasted chocolate. When he finally pulled back, they were both breathing hard. But if they had caught anyone's attention, it was the kiss they would see, not her full body spasm.

His fingers were still inside of her. Her pussy pulsing with its pleasure as he slowly pulled them out. Chloe could only lay there limply and watch as he sucked her juices off his fingers. When he had thoroughly sucked them clean, he smiled at her.

"Your place or mine?"

CHAPTER THREE: CHLOE & DAEVON

The reason Chloe took him to her place was because it kept things in her control. She wasn't the one that would have to put on their clothes and leave, doing the walk of shame in the morning. That is, if she let him stay until morning. Usually, it was more like a couple of times with the intercourse and then the guy would be too tired to continue. As soon as a male petered out - so to speak - she had no more use for him. She liked sleeping alone. So, bye, bye, and lock the door behind him so she could shower and go to bed. Once she had her engine revved a couple of times, it didn't matter how little sleep she got, she was raring to go in the morning.

Daevon didn't comment about her being on the penthouse floor. Usually, guys talked about how impressed they were as soon as she used her key and pushed the button. Daevon pulled her into his arms and kissed her thoroughly. His lips were soft and firm. He nibbled her lips with his and not his teeth. He kissed the corners of her mouth before sucking her bottom lip between his and sucking gently.

The ding from the elevator was loud as they reached the penthouse floor. And the doors slid open almost soundlessly.

Releasing her bottom lip, he looked deeply into her eyes before scooping her up into his arms and carrying her out of the elevator to the right to her front door. She couldn't take her eyes off him. He had a handsome face, yes, with strong features, a square chin with a slight dimple, a perfectly straight nose, deep-set eyes, and brows that curved naturally. But given as a whole, he was more handsome than Sidney Pointier, Michael B. Jordan, or even a young Billy Dee Williams.

"Thumbprint," Daevon uttered in that incredible voice. It took a moment before it sank in.

"Oh," Chloe replied in almost a dream state. "Oh!" she remarked as she realized what he was saying. She reached over from the comfort of his arms and placed her thumb on the digital access panel on the door, springing open the entry way. He carried her inside.

The spell broken; Chloe made as if she was getting down.

"No, not yet" Daevon intoned as he carried her to her bedroom as if he knew the way. The lights had automatically turned on as soon as the door opened, but he was nibbling her earlobe and not watching the direction he was going like he'd done this a thousand times before. For some reason, this made her feel unsettled. Not that she expected him to be a virgin and God knew - she wasn't. Him having lovemaking skills was a big bonus. But she felt like he was in control and that unnerved her.

He went down with her as he laid her on her kind-sized bed. He was kissing her again, making her lose her damned mind as his hand slid down one of her legs and removed her four-inch stiletto from that foot.

She heard it hit the floor and didn't care as his warm, wet tongue began to explore her mouth with a loving gentleness she could never remember a man using. Getting her mouth fucked with a hard tongue was usually a guy's standard operating procedure. Men always thought that they had to choke you out with their tongue. But this was dreamy. This was delish. This was heating up her whole body to a nuclear level.

The other shoe hit the floor to join its sister.

She got with the program and found his tie, loosening it from his throat. She tossed it in the general area as the sisters. They rolled around on the bed, undressing each other, kissing, and tonguing each other, clothes flying in all directions until she was down to her silk bra and panties, and he was down to his black boxers that looked like they were housing a grain silo.

Damn, Chloe thought to herself, was that man even going to fit?

She rolled him to his back and hooked her fingers into the waistband of those boxers and pulled them down his muscled legs while her eyes stayed locked on his cock.

He. Was. Huge.

How could a geek with an electronics company look like that?

"Like what you see," he intoned in the Barry White voice as he smiled at her.

"Yes," she whispered, still staring at that Empire State Building.

Snapping out of it, she tossed his boxers over her shoulder and moved down the bed to his ankles. Both her hands slowly glided over his ankles and just below his shins as she alternated between kissing, licking and gently biting his skin that her hands were massaging.

Daevon lifted himself to his elbows and watched her. Women generally whooped and hollered over his cock and then climbed aboard. But not her. His cock was raising its hand, saying: "Hey, up here!" It was pulsating so hard he could see his heartbeat in it. She was moving up to his calves and shins now. New sensations were now overtaking him. He laid back down and closed his eyes, concentrating on the feelings.

The anticipation was exotic and frustrating. He couldn't wait for her to do to his cock what she was doing to his legs. Now she added her nails to the mix. Scraping along his skin just enough to create a new sensation, but not enough to draw blood. When she got to the top of his thighs, she used her hands under his knees to part his legs wide. He popped his eyes open to watch what she was going to do next.

Now that he was spread wide, Chloe reached up to his chest with those nails and slowly pulled them down over his pecs, down his torso, over his belly, to his groin, completely avoiding his cock, and down to the tops of his thighs again. As his cock wept a pearl of clear liquid at its tip, Chloe pursed her lips and gently blew across the top of his bulging head.

"Stop teasing me, woman," he groaned, loudly. But he loved it. Finally, a woman who saw him as a whole man and not just a big cock. But yeah, he did have a big cock.

Chloe's eyes focused on that huge sac that hung below his weeping cock. She blew on it softly. He groaned again. She began licking that sac like it was a chocolate ice cream cone, making sure none of it melted. Then she sucked one side of the sac into her mouth until she could feel his left ball in her mouth. Then she sucked and licked it while it was still in her mouth.

He. Went. Wild.

Groaning. Lifting up on his elbows again. Collapsing back. Covering his face with his hands. She slowly pulled back until his ball came popping out, snapping back into place. Then she did the same thing to the other side.

He couldn't take it anymore. As soon as she let his right ball plop back into place, he sat up, reached down, and pulled her body up his. Flipping her around so he was now on top, he gathered up her legs with muscled arms and slipped them up over his shoulders.

His fingers moved aside her soaking-wet panties and his huge cock spread her swollen pussy lips like butter, yielding to him all her wet, wonderful juices. They both groaned loudly as he buried himself deep.

Yeah. He fit, Chloe thought to herself. She was so wet and ready, he probably could have driven a Buick into her, and it would fit, she wanted him so badly. He still hadn't moved though. He may be huge, but she was tight. No pregnancies and hours of working out kept her tight like a dancer's body.

"Baby," he said breathlessly, "I gotta cum. I promise I'll make it up to you," the look on his face both agony and earnestness.

"You go, baby," she smiled up at him as he held himself up with those bulging arms. "Just don't plan on sleeping tonight," she gave him a naughty grin.

He gave a half-laugh and then began to pump. The suction of her pussy on his cock refused to let go, and he was groaning on each and every thrust. She held on to his huge biceps as he rocked her thoroughly. Suddenly going wild, he pounded into her. Chloe had to release her hold on him and put her hands up against the headboard to keep her head from knocking into it.

He. Came. HARD.

She. Came HARD.

Their shouts and yells were so loud that Chloe was sure they were heard all the way down to the gym.

Daevon collapsed on her and then quickly rolled them both to their sides while he kept them connected. To make sure they stayed that way, Chloe took her top leg and wrapped it around his ass. They were both breathing as if they just finished a marathon. She drew one long lick up his throat with her tongue, enjoying the salty taste of him.

Suddenly, her breasts had more room to move. He had unhooked her bra, and she hadn't felt him doing it. To help, she pulled her bra off and threw it to the floor with everything else that was setting up camp there. Daevon groaned, moved back a little, and swept up one gorgeous round breast into his hand and kneaded it gently. After a few moments, he moved down, and his cock pulled out of her.

Although it had been emptied, his was still big. Chloe liked that. It promised more.

Daevon was now licking and sucking her nipple as his hand left that breast and moved to the other. His lips gently plucked on her nipple to mimic the gentle plucking his thumb and forefinger was doing with the other nipple. He switched back and forth. One nipple plucked and massaged by his fingers while his mouth did the same with the other. He then gathered them both up in his hands and rubbed his face all over them.

"Baby, you're just too much," he whispered as he moved down her body, whipped off her panties, and threw those to the floor as well.

He then treated her to the same workout she had given him. The ankles. The calves and shins. The knees. The thighs. He split her legs wide and ran his hands down her neck, breasts, stomach, and groin, completely ignoring her ready sex. Her sex was not pleased. She was amused, however. And enjoying the sensations of him all over her as he repeated the whole thing again. He gently bit the insides of her thighs. He blew on her nether lips. She was whining and panting now. He slipped her legs over his shoulders, put his hands on the backs of her thighs to hold her in place, and began licking her wet sex as if it were the chocolate mousse from the restaurant.

"Jesus God!" she screamed as she came. But he didn't stop. He kept tonguing her as if he knew every one of her places, all her weaknesses. "Jesus!" she groaned as his tongue rode her hard.

She came again.

And again.

And again.

Her bones were jelly by the time he had finished. She just laid there like she was a melted puddle, the jerks and vibrations of her climaxes streaking through her, slowly winding down.

He allowed her a few moments more rest, and then he rearranged her limbs and filled her with his heavy cock again. This time he used a slow movement that brought his cock out almost to its tip and then pushed back in until her pelvis was against his. Over and over, he controlled his strokes, bringing both along at the same time. She was thrusting her hips up to meet his, mewling and groaning for release. She tried to increase his speed by ramming up onto him. But he was determined to make her come before him. Her own hands went to her breasts, and she started playing with her nipples, twisting them gently, pulling softly until she was really pulling hard on them and kneading her own tits like bread. He was kissing and biting her lips, pulling her bottom lip out gently with his teeth.

"Fuck me, goddamn it!" she yelled as she pulled her mouth away. He smiled and then grabbed her hips and pulled them up with him as he got on his knees, keeping them together. He started fucking her hard. Her legs went beside his head, and she squeezed to hold on. Her hands went back to the headboard because he was fucking her body up toward it again.

"Yes!" she screamed as she came. "Yes, yes, fuck me hard!"

"Oh, shit! Oh shit! Fuck, yes!" he hollered back as he exploded inside her. Along with the gripping sensations from her own pumping vagina, Chloe deliberately tightened and release her passage to drive him crazy further.

"Oh, man!" he breathed as she continued to milk his cock. He suddenly pulled out, flipped her around and pulled her up on all fours. His big cock was in her quickly again and he held her hips and he plunged in and out of her. His sac kept rocking up and slapping her groin from the momentum.

"Fuck, yes!" they both shouted at the same time as Chloe looked between her breasts at his sac slapping her, her breasts flapping back and forth, Daevon tightly gripping her hips as his dick fucked her harder. At just the right moment, he took one of his hands off her hip and slipped his little finger into her ass.

She exploded.

Her scream on a level that Moscow could hear. And then she began to cry. Chloe curled into a ball as he removed his cock and finger. Daevon quickly pulled up the duvet and covered her. He wrapped his body around hers and slowly rubbed her back with his large hand. Occasionally, he placed a kiss on the back of her neck while he let her drift.

Chloe didn't know how long it took her to recover. She just went with it. His kisses and massages, his big body curled around hers letting her know she was safe. That he wouldn't let anything disturb her. As she started to surface again, her eyes finally dry, she realized that he hadn't cum. Turning in his arms, she looked at him.

"What about you?" she asked.

"Don't worry 'bout me; you take all the time you need," he whispered.

"I'm fine now. It's your turn," she gave him a mischievous smile as she threw off the duvet, the silk in it causing it to slip off the bed and onto the floor. Chloe pushed him to his back and got between his legs. His cock was not disappointing. It was still rigid with expectation. She began by licking his cock from balls to tip, causing him to groan. Her hands kneaded his ball sac gently while her mouth and tongue went to work on his head. After several moments, she switched, and her hands kneaded his weeping head, and her mouth was at his sac. Soon, he was gasping. Begging. His breath was forced in and out. Soon, with her hands, one after the other, in the middle of cock, she twisted each fist the opposite way of the other. Her fist on the top twisting up the shaft, and her hand on the bottom twisting down. They moved the opposite way of each other, so the length of that big fat cock was attended to.

"Jesus!" Daevon blurted out. "Jesus, god! Oh, baby!"

As Daevon grabbed up the sheets in his fists, he started to come. Chloe was on it, stretching her mouth around that enormous head, letting his hot juice fire into her mouth. She swallowed. And swallowed.

And swallowed.

She continued to milk him dry, lapping up any of that warm salty juice that escaped. Pretty soon, he was too sensitive there, and his hands were on her shoulders, trying to ease her back as his eyes rolled back into his head. She sat up and watched him shutter with his climax as she licked her lips. Suddenly, Daevon sat up quickly, wrapped her in his arms, and brought her down on top of his chest as they lay together. With the warmth of their bodies together, they slept.

CHAPTER FOUR: CHLOE & DAEVON

Chloe woke to soft kisses on her face. Her eyes fluttered open and Daevon smiled that beautiful way of his at her. She smiled back, closing her eyes and stretching as the satisfied, contented cat that she was.

"You hungry?" he asked as she stretched in another direction. "Should we send a concierge out for something?" She opened her eyes and grinned.

"Fuck that. My butler cooks stuff for me ahead of time and freezes it. How do enchiladas sound?"

"Fan - dam - tastic," he exclaimed with enthusiasm.

"You start the shower, and I'll load the oven," she directed as she rose out of bed. His greedy eyes gave her a long up-and-down look, and she gave her a great view of her ass as she bent down, picked up his shirt, and put it on. His long arm snapped out to grab her, but she evaded his grasp with a giggle as she went to the door. "Shower first!" she teased as she wagged her finger at him.

"Yes, boss," he replied, grinning.

"And don't forget that!" she teased as she put on a stern look.

Chloe was floating on air as she made her way to the kitchen, the lights in the house coming on as she walked through the rooms. She opened her floor to ceiling freezer and found the enchiladas. Reading the note attached as she closed the freezer, she moved it to the large kitchen island.

"Oven," she began, "preheat at three-hundred-fifty degrees for five minutes.

"Preheating oven at three hundred fifty degrees for five minutes," a feminine voice responded. Chloe set the note aside and popped the large tray of enchiladas into the oven.

"Oven, kitchen timer for one hour."

"Would you like that kitchen timer set for one hour after the five-minute preheat timer?"

"Yes, please," Chloe tossed over her shoulder as she left the kitchen.

"Setting kitchen timer," the feminine voice replied.

Chloe knew she should wait those five minutes before putting her pan in the oven, but she had something better waiting for her in the shower. She walked through the dark bedroom as she removed his shirt. This time, however, she tossed it on the bed instead of the floor. She could hear the water running in the bathroom as she made her way there. Opening the door, the air was warm and steamy. The lights had been set to low. Enough to see and still be romantic. Daevon's huge form was behind the foggy glass of the shower.

Chloe sighed. Damn, she thought to herself, he was such delicious eye candy. No, a little voice in the back of her head said. He is much more than that.

But she didn't want to think about that right now. This was jungle gym time. This was fun time.

Daevon had used his time in the shower to thoroughly clean himself. He washed his hair with her shampoo, used her conditioner, and soaped it up with some righteous-smelling soap that he just had to find out what it was so he could get some of his own. He wanted to be clean when Chloe got back so he could concentrate completely on her.

And then, there she was. Beautifully naked, her high round beasts bobbing gently as she opened the glass shower door and came in to him.

Instant hard-on.

Baseball bat.

Rocket ship.

Mount Vesuvius.

Dodge Ram truck.

Whatever metaphor you wanted to use; he was rocking it. Her eyes went immediately to his cock and stayed there. She smiled like she was going to burgle something - and - knew she would get away with it. Hands in the cookie jar time. She sank to her knees in front of him, the water hitting the back of her head, and he practically came right there and then. Just seeing her poised between his—-

"Oh, fuck!" he barked as she grabbed his cock and sucked him into her mouth. As her mouth stretched and worked out his rigid member, her hands went for his sac and separated his balls, kneading them gently and slowly while her head pistoned back and forth as she swallowed him in.

Talk about hands-free.

His hands automatically went to her head, and he held her gently and he helped her with some hip action of his own. He was careful not to hold too tightly. He didn't want her to feel trapped or feel she couldn't stop if she wanted. Even though her mouth was spread wide to accommodate him, she was having no trouble swallowing a good deal of him. Something that came with a lot of practice.

He didn't want to think about that. This was their time together. Just the two of them, and there were no virgins in this shower.

Chloe let go of his balls and did the hands-twisting-opposite of each other on his cock skin again, and he—

There she blows!

Or there he blows.

His hot cream fired into her mouth so fast she really had to swallow over and over again to take it all in. As he fell back against the shower wall, she opened her lips so she wouldn't hurt him as he popped out of her mouth. Looking at his heavy-lidded eyes, she licked her lips slowly and completely. Then she turned demurely to the shower and picked up her shampoo.

He watched her measure out a quarter-sized amount of shampoo, flip the lid closed and put it back in the holder. She rubbed her hands together before sending them into her tresses to soap them up. He guessed he used too much shampoo when he did his own hair.

He slipped his fingers into her hair and took over washing it for her. She relaxed her arms and enjoyed his ministrations. Since her hands were soapy, she rubbed them over her breasts and belly. He continued the suds down to her shoulders and massaged them and then her back. Her head fell back against his chest, allowing him a look at those gorgeous tits. His hands automatically went over her shoulders and down to those magnificent globes. Even though she had already done it, he soaped them up good - really good - pausing at the nipples to tease them. His hard-on was roaring back to life as he watched himself play with her breasts.

Chloe moved forward and began rinsing herself thoroughly. Disappointed to be separated from her flesh, he went to her. Daevon helped her get the shampoo out of her hair, once again wondering how she was able to get her hair so straight and long. When her hair was free of suds, he helped her squeeze out the extra water. She then went for the conditioner, placing only a dime-sized drop in her palm.

Damn.

He really had overused the conditioner. Did this mean he was going to slide right off the mattress when they hit the bed again?

She rubbed her palms together again and then picked through her hair, barely putting the conditioner on. She did that for several minutes, and he just watched, intrigued by the Spartan use of the same items he'd used. When it was clear that she had lightly tapped all over her head, she rubbed her palms together again, gathered her hair in her palms, and slowly pulled it through.

"Now, I like to let that sit for about five minutes. Do you have any ideas about what we can do in the meantime?" she asked naughtily.

Hell yeah.

Daevon leaned down and gathered her up until her sex was in his face and her legs draped over his shoulders. She squealed as he picked her up, and Chloe put one hand on top of the shower door to hold on, and the other went flat on the wall for support. He began sucking and licking her clit like she was tender, juicy fruit he could never get enough of.

Chloe wound her ankles around his torso for more support and then began riding his face like he was her favorite horse. He held her up by her ass cheeks as he used his entire face to get her off. When she seemed to level off, not being able to reach her climax, he stuck two fingers in her sex and fucked her while his mouth worked on the button at the top of her clit. It wasn't long before her arms were wrapped around his head, and she moaned loud enough to raise the roof.

"Yes! Yes, right there! Get it! Get it, baby! That's right! Eat me! Eat me! Oh, yeah!" And then she screamed and shuttered. She riled up sex and actually squirted her juice into his mouth. He lapped up her salty sauce and then let her slide down his body, guiding her with his hands. She clung to him, her shivers and tremors reaching him through the touch of her body to his.

Daevon turned his face to the running water and cleaned her come off his face. His big hands stroked her back softly and slowly, up and down, as he allowed her to enjoy all of her climax. He felt a sensation at his chest. Looking down, he saw that she had taken his nipple into her lips, and she was sucking on it. Next, her hand took hold of his cock, and she began stroking it. He let his head drop back, and he closed his eyes. She switched over to his other nipple and drove him crazy with the sensation of her plucking it with her taunt lips. His cock was loving the attention too. He hated to put a halt to any of it, but he wanted the bed for the next round. Reaching over, he shut off the shower.

"Why'd you do that?" as she pulled back to look at him.

Instead of answering, he lifted her in his arms and carried her out of the shower over to a padded seat in front of a mirror and sat her down on it. He pulled a towel off the rack and began drying her hair. She made concentration difficult by taking hold of his cock again and continuing her stroking. Once he had secured the towel around her head, he pulled another towel over and began drying her all over. Pretty soon, however, he had to free his cock from her hand, or he was going to unload all over her clean skin. Wrapping her in that towel, he carried her to the bed and laid her down.

"Don't move," he cautioned, pointing his finger at her. "I'll be right back." Returning to the bathroom, he quickly toweled off his body and his hair. He went back into the bedroom and found her naked on the bed, the towels discarded.

"I'm not good at following orders," she teased as she spread her legs wide.

"I think I'll forgive you," he purred, and he climbed onto the bed and over her, his large arms holding him above her.

"Stick it in, baby," she purred back as she took her hands, gathered up her breasts, and pushed them together.

He thrust into her and embedded himself deeply without even looking. They both groaned as he found home. Daevon lowered himself to his elbows and began plunging into and out of her body like he was a well-oiled machine. His mouth found her nipples as she continued to hold her titties together for him.

"That's it, baby. Fuck me. Yeah, you know how I like it. I love that big cock of yours. It owns me. That's right, fuck that, baby. Yeah, you know it," she encouraged. The dirty talk drove him to a quick climax. As he started to come, she quickly added, "Own me baby. Yeah, make me your own. Mark it! mark me, baby. Shoot that hot juice of yours all over me." So, he did. He pulled out, his cock pumping out his juice. He grabbed his cock to aim it and he pumped himself at the same time. He covered her clit. Her belly. Her tits. She held them up for him so he could reach under them as well. Then she leaned her head forward, opened her mouth wide and stuck out her tongue like she was getting ready to lick an ice cream cone. He shot his come into her mouth. He was so excited by her wanting him all over him, he seemed to have an unlimited amount of sauce. Then she surprised him by closing her mouth and eyes and putting her face right into his pumping stream until her face was covered. He was finally out of juice. And wrung out as well. He rolled over and laid beside her as she used her hands to rub in all his come. He was breathing hard, despite his excellent physical condition, which simply told him he'd had quite a workout. If he'd known that, he might have skipped the gym. Of course, if he had, he wouldn't have met her. Maybe he'd skip the gym tomorrow.

"Ejaculate is filled with vitamin D and is very good for the skin," she purred as his breathing slowed. He rolled toward her and stayed on his side as he held his head up with a big palm.

"Is that so?" he smiled. "Did it curb your appetite for those enchiladas?"

"Never!" she grinned. Like that, she was off the bed and heading into the bathroom. She gave him a saucy look over her shoulder as she went to the sink, wet a washcloth, and cleaned herself. Getting off the bed, too, Daevon slipped on his black boxers and went out toward the kitchen, the lights turning on as he went. When he got to the kitchen, he looked for and found two oven mitts and tried to fit his big hands into them. No luck. He used them as hot pads, opened the oven, reached in with them, and took out the enchiladas. As he set them on top of the stove, the appliance spoke to him.

"The timer finished so I have kept the oven on warm for five minutes, thirty-four seconds."

"Thank you," he replied as he folded back the foil on top of the hot dish.

"You're welcome," the appliance answered cheerfully.

"You're not coming on to my stove, are you?" Chloe smiled as she went to the cupboard and removed two plates.

"Caught me," he teased as he found the silverware drawer after previously trying two other drawers.

Chloe snagged a stainless-steel spatula and began serving up the enchiladas. Daevon opened the refrigerator. He snagged a couple of beers and shut the door. She took the plates and silverware to the table; he brought the beer and a napkin holder. Chloe went back to the fridge as he sat down and found two types of hot sauce. Shutting the door, she took them to the table and sat down.

"Hot. And hotter," she pronounced as she set them in front of him.

He took the second bottle and put some on the side of his plate.

"Chicken?" she asked.

"Cautious," he replied. They both laughed as he twisted the tops off of the beers and handed her one. They clinked bottlenecks and drank a little before digging into their meal.

CHAPTER FIVE: CHLOE & DAEVON

The next morning as Chloe worked through her day, she was extremely irritated, and she wasn't talking about chaffed thighs or a tired vagina. Daevon had left sometime in the night and not even said goodbye.

She had awoken alone. No notes left anywhere.

No text messages.

Not even a phone call.

Of course, she couldn't hold that against him because she hadn't given him her number. But that was no excuse! She could freaking hold it against him!

Then she had walked into a disaster at work. The computer servers were down. Her tech guys had worked on it without much luck before calling in some Big Guns. She couldn't stand by waiting while the business world scurried by. Who did she have to blow to get her company back up and running?

When she thought about blowing and getting up, she immediately thought about Daevon. Man, that was some huge cock he had hanging from his pelvis. And his stamina. F-U-C-K! She drew the word out in her mind. She was sitting behind her glass desk and felt the need to re-cross her legs, one over the other, from the way they were now. Her sex was throbbing just thinking about that man.

After their enchilada meal, they had cleaned up the kitchen together - even though the butler would be there in the morning. They chatted and laughed. They had compared notes: neither had been married; they were too busy with their companies for a serious relationship; both were only children; both had lost their virginities at early ages. He at fourteen, her at sixteen. They had both lost their fathers to illness. And they both took care of their mothers, paying for their condos at the seniors' country club where their moms played golf and a variety of card games, swam in the pool, worked out in the senior gym, dined at the clubhouse dining hall and went to movie nights. It was a small world in which their moms were in the same place, but it was the best one in the state, and when it came to their moms, they spared no expense.

By the time they had gone back to bed, the air between them felt different. Chloe felt a sort of bond due to having had so many things in common. They made love differently as well. It was very tender. They spent a great deal of time just kissing. They were holding each other more. They looked into one another eyes more, not just where their bodies were connected. For the first time in her life, Chloe didn't feel like she was playing on a jungle gym but was making love with a man. For a few seconds, Chloe allowed herself to think this might be something special.

Then that sonofabitch left without a word. Without a fucking word!

When Chloe rode up in the elevator that night, she felt like she had a ton of bar bells on her shoulders. She didn't feel like working out or doing anything close to her usual routine.

The elevator dinged, the doors opened, and she walked out and turned right, walking down to her apartment door. She touched the pad with her thumb, and the door swung open. Stepping in, she—

"Oh, my god!" she exclaimed when she looked around the apartment. Roses of every color were everywhere. And then there was every kind of lily. And then she saw the orchids. Beautiful, beautiful orchids. Each of the flower types was in its own crystal vase and arranged around the room in clusters of three, one of each kind in a trio.

"Good evening, Miss," her butler Lester intoned as he gave a curt nod of his head toward her. I've taken the liberty of arranging the flowers. I hope it meets with Miss's approval." He extended an envelope toward her. She took it.

"When did these come?" she asked as she opened the envelope.

"Just after Miss left this morning," he answered as he fussed with a couple of blooms.

Chloe read the card to herself. 'Hey Beautiful. Thanks for last night. I've been called away.'

"I've been called away," she repeated out loud. "Called away. Well, that's a new version of, 'it's not you, it's me', if I've ever heard it!"

"Would Miss like me to prepare some dinner?" the butler asked.

"No. What I want is for you to throw all these away!" She ripped the envelope up.

"Miss?" balked the butler, saucer-eyed. "They are very expensive," he finished flummoxed.

"Fine! Give them to a hospital or an old folk's home - just get them out of my sight!" She stomped off to her bedroom and slammed the door.

"And I thought that messy bed meant that they'd had a good time last night," Lester mumbled under his breath.

In her room, Chloe threw the envelope pieces into the air so they rained down on her like ticker tape. She then ripped off her clothes as if she were punishing them. "Thanks for last night. Babe," she said in a snotty voice. She tossed her shoes in the general direction. of the closet. "Oh, yeah, and I've been called away!" She shimmied out of her pencil skirt and stomped on it as she whipped her silk blouse over her head and tossed it at a chair. "Thanks, babe! Sorry to fuck and run, babe!" She thought of that Beatles song Admiral Halsey and uttered a particular line: "Cuz we're so e-a-s-i-l-y called away!" Wearing only her bra and panties, she threw herself across her big bed, so she landed on her back. There was no sense in getting under the covers; the butler had surely changed the sheets so they weren't going to smell like Daevon. They'd be fresh, crisp, and spring-like.

Of course, she didn't want them to smell like him. She wasn't trying to remember what he smelled like. Felt like. Tasted like. She wasn't. No. She absolutely wasn't. Just fucking wasn't! Damn it!

The next morning at work, her tech guys told her that the "Big Gun" they had called in said he'd have her servers up and running by noon that day. Well, it was now eleven-forty-fucking-five 'A' of the 'M', so he'd better fucking hurry, she thought to herself.

Looking up from her desk, Chloe saw Daevon right outside the glass wall of her office. He smiled and briefly waved his hand before pulling open the door and walking in.

She stood up quickly.

"Hey, baby," he said quietly.

"Don't you, hey baby me," she glared at him as she crossed her arms over her chest.

"Oh, sorry," he continued quietly. "I know it's your place of business, that's why I didn't say it loudly. Didn't want to disrespect you at your company."

"But you have no problem taking off on me in the middle of the night without so much as a goodbye!" she said more loudly than him, but she still kept it between them. It was bad enough that the entire office could see them in here together. For the first time, she wasn't so thrilled about having an all-glass office. Or plexiglass. Or whatever the fuck - who cared? How dare he come here like it was just another day!

"Well, first of all," he began with that Barry White tone in at a normal conversation level, "it wasn't the middle of the night. It was four a.m. And secondly, I did say goodbye. I kissed you all over your face until you woke up."

Her breath almost caught in her throat. But she was not going to give in so easily to his Barry-fucking-White voice. "Funny how I don't remember that," she said. "You sure I was awake?"

"Yeah, you said, hey my teddy bear, where ya goin'?"

"I. Did. Not!" I've never referred to anyone as 'my teddy bear' - ever!" she huffed. "If I ever gave you a pet name, it would be more along the lines of: 'Big cock of the walk', 'Cock of Gibraltar', "Mount Cock' - not 'teddy bear'. Pul-eeze!" His grin infuriated her. "What are you smiling about?"

"I swear it was teddy bear. I'm not making this up." He tried to reign in his grin, but it was a fight for him. "Although I do appreciate the nom de plumes."

"What are you doing here, anyway?" She uncrossed her arms and put her hands on her hips.

"Solving your server problems. And I did it before noon, just like I said I would." He looked very satisfied.

"Wait. You're the one they called?"

"Yep. And when I found out it was your company, I put my best guys on it. Including myself. Can't have my lady's company down."

"That's where you were called away?"

"Yep. Did you get my flowers?"

"Flowers... Uh, yeah. But I knew I wouldn't be home to appreciate them so..."

"So?" he asked as he moved his head around, trying to look into her eyes which were avoiding looking at him.

"So, I had my butler take them to the old folks' home and the hospital so others could enjoy them." At least, she hoped that's what he'd done.

His knowing look irritated her beyond belief. If he kept this up, it wouldn't be long before he'd be on her last nerve.

"So, my Queen," he began moving toward her slowly, like a liquid flowing smoothly. Are we going to make this official? Or are you going to keep on pretending to be mad at me, thinking that will keep me at bay?"

Her eyes were riveted on him. Her body heated up with each step he took. He was right. They both knew they couldn't pretend. Just one look, and they each lit up like a bonfire. Their bodies wanted each other - needed each other. She could deny it all she wanted - but she was only fooling herself.

Just as he reached her, Chloe jumped up into his arms. He grabbed her by the ass and hoisted her up high on his chest, and they kissed each other for all they were worth. Wanting to look graceful while they tongued the hell out of each other, Chloe bent her knees and crossed her legs at her ankles as she leaned into him. They could hear her employees clapping on the other side of the glass wall of her office. When they finally came up for air, Daevon smiled at her.

"Why don't we go back to my place and practice making a baby?"

"But - I'm on the pill!" she gave him a worried look.

"I said practice," he grinned.

She slapped him playfully on the chin and kissed him again.

-—END—-

Don't miss out!

Visit the website below and you can sign up to receive emails whenever Jordan Rivers publishes a new book. There's no charge and no obligation.

https://books2read.com/r/B-A-YHHHB-SRLCD

Connecting independent readers to independent writers.

Also by Jordan Rivers

Hunky Nerd Series
Hunky Nerd 1 & 2

Standalone
A Duchess's Redemption
Víspera de brujas
Witches' Eve
The Five Suitors
Empowered Survival: A Comprehensive Guide For Women
The Weekend Fisherman's Cookbook
Easy Fitness for Seniors
High Desert
How to Train for the Combine
Alto Desierto
Supervivencia Empoderada: ung guia completa para mujeres

About the Author

I started writing for fun when I was a kid but I didn't get serious about publishing until my 20s. After taking film and broadcasting in college I felt I'd found my true calling. I now write, direct, and produce ultra-low-budget movies. I've won two awards for my scripts; editor's choice for poetry and I'm published in paperback as well on Amazon. My first non-fiction book entitled, "I Know How You Feel..." is about my ten-year struggle with the death of my oldest son and how writing about it brought me back.